RAZORBILL

CROSS MY HEART

CROSS MY HEART

Sasha Gould

razor
bill

PENGUIN

RAZORBILL

Published by the Penguin Group

Penguin Books Ltd, 80 Strand, London WC2R ORL, England

Penguin Group (USA) Inc., 375 Hudson Street, New York, New York 10014, USA

Penguin Group (Canada), 90 Eglinton Avenue East, Suite 700, Toronto, Ontario, Canada M4P 2Y3
(a division of Pearson Penguin Canada Inc.)

Penguin Ireland, 25 St Stephen's Green, Dublin 2, Ireland (a division of Penguin Books Ltd)

Penguin Group (Australia), 250 Camberwell Road, Camberwell, Victoria 3124, Australia
(a division of Pearson Australia Group Pty Ltd)

Penguin Books India Pvt Ltd, 11 Community Centre, Panchsheel Park, New Delhi – 110 017, India

Penguin Group (NZ), 67 Apollo Drive, Rosedale, Auckland 0632, New Zealand
(a division of Pearson New Zealand Ltd)

Penguin Books (South Africa) (Pty) Ltd, 24 Sturdee Avenue, Rosebank,
Johannesburg 2196, South Africa

Penguin Books Ltd, Registered Offices: 80 Strand, London WC2R ORL, England

penguin.com

First published 2011
001 – 10 9 8 7 6 5 4 3 2 1

Series created by Working Partners Ltd, London
Text copyright © Working Partners Ltd 2011
All rights reserved

Set in Bembo Book MT Std 11.5/15.5 pt
Typeset by Palimpsest Book Production Limited, Falkirk, Stirlingshire
Printed in Great Britain by Clays Ltd, St Ives plc

British Library Cataloguing in Publication Data
A CIP catalogue record for this book is available from the British Library

ISBN: 978-0-141-33392-2

www.greenpenguin.co.uk

With special thanks to Sarah Moore Fitzgerald

Prologue

His gondola slips through the water like a knife cutting into dark silk. The two passengers rustle and laugh, but from where he's standing he can't really see what they're up to. It's none of his concern if some rich old gentleman wants to pay for favours from a young beauty – even if she is some other father's daughter.

He sighs, pulls his oar against the water and slows to a stop. Wordlessly he helps them both on to the street. For a second he looks straight into the eyes of the man, taking payment, and then the improbable couple sweeps off, the man's shoes clacking quickly on the stone, the girl's laughter floating up into the night. Their steps echo down the lane past St Mark's Square.

His gondola shines and flashes in the moonlight as he starts to make his way home. He steers it with the skill of generations, gliding by the looming palazzos, slanting and turning past St Zulian, St Salvador and Mazzini – along back canals that draw their convoluted chart from St Mark's to the Rialto Bridge. It's a confusing network, full of false turns and unexpected hazards – easy to get lost, especially at night. Unless you're a gondolier, in which case you know these watery alleys like the lines on your own face.

He's close to home when he hears it: a long and awful scream that fills the night. There's splashing too and someone bangs a stick on a rail. He rounds a corner and sees an old woman running up and down the bank, begging for help, still wailing. High above, shutters creak open. A voice thick with sleep throatily demands an end to the commotion. Curious faces lean from the frames of weakly lit windows.

At first he thinks that what he sees in the water is a sheet or a curtain – a swollen soggy dome bobbing gently in the blackness. He drifts closer and sees that it's a dress that breaks the surface. A woman. Shoeless and face down. She floats near enough the edge to be pulled to the bank by his oar. With the help of the old woman, he hauls her body on to the stone verge. He's aware of the people gathering in a ring around them. Slowly, heavily, he turns her over.

It is a girl, perhaps twenty. Soft fingers, now cold. Lips, already blue. In life she must have been exquisite. The eyes are half open, staring limpidly at the sky.

The old woman's wails become deeper. First she falls beside the body, pulling strands of wet hair from the dead face. Then she stands up and clutches at him with bony hands, wetly clinging to his jacket. 'God help me, God help her. Jesus, God in heaven, do something for us!'

He takes the woman's hands and holds them for a moment in his. To the onlookers, it could seem like a gesture of comfort or care. But really it's his effort to disentangle himself from all this panic and grief. 'Signora. I'm sorry, signora, but there's no helping her now,' he says, and slips away.

1

None of us is known by our real name in here. Almost as soon as you arrive, you're christened all over again: La Grossa, La Cadavara, La Lunatica, La Trista, La Puera, La Pungenta – Fat, Deathly, Mad, Sad, Fearful and Stinky. Inside the walls of the convent, sneering adjectives are transformed, sooner or later, into names.

They call me La Muta – The Silent One. It isn't that I don't have plenty to say, it's just that most of the time I keep things to myself. Daughters learn this early. Second daughters sooner.

The Abbess used to tell me that she could see something feral in my soul – that there was something of the animal about me. A dog, perhaps, or maybe a rat. The creatures that slip into the convent at night in search of chicken bones and rotting food. It's something that she's determined to stamp out.

My life, which once belonged to my father, now belongs to her. I am awake before two for prayers and then again at five, to go and sing perfect harmonies as the Venetian sun rises behind the grilles and the bars, dancing on the marble and gold in the chapel.

The Abbess controls all the correspondence coming in and

going out. Sometimes she withholds the letters from my sister Beatrice and I can't read them. *Tell me your news*, I'd beg Beatrice in writing. *When will you marry Vincenzo? Does he make you happy?* None of my questions can be asked without the prudish scrutiny of the Abbess. To a suspicious mind, alert to all possible evils, any of my words could somehow appear saturated with sin.

'I see everything,' the Abbess tells me. 'I know what is in your mind.'

I used to believe her. I used to think that perhaps she really did have the power to see my secret longings leaking like olive oil from the press. Certainly, I've seen her holding our letters out in front of her by the corners as if there's a danger they'll smear her cowl or habit. As if they're greasy, grubby things.

Some of Beatrice's letters reach me. I hide them in a blue wooden box with my own ring and with a silk-ribboned lock of her hair. Late at night, when Annalena is snoring and shifting under her sheets, I take my sister's folded ink-papered treasures and I read them again and again. Each of her letters carries something from the outside world, smuggling it inside these walls that separate us. Through nothing but an accident of birth, she remains free, while I languish.

Annalena is my *conversa*, my lay sister, my servant nun, and she teases me for smiling in my sleep. She says my eyelids flutter and she wonders what worlds I'm travelling to in the dark.

In my dreams I'm a child again. Beatrice and I are running down to the Lido for treats from Paulina's grandmother. Paulina – my friend without a father. It always saddened me that her papa had died when he was young, but now I wonder whether she might actually be blessed, living as she did, alone with her mother. Her grandmama shrouded her body in black clothes and the skin on her face was hard and grooved like the folds of a walnut.

'The little princesses,' she would call us. And she would lisp, '*Shhh!*' and say 'Don't tell your papa you were here.' And as she looked at our faces she would gasp, 'Oh, what husbands you'll have! What riches! How many men will long to touch your skin and to comb your hair with their fingers!'

She had a bakery, and in the summer, when she couldn't bear the heat of the ovens, she would let them cool down and make nothing but meringues. She was famous for them. The recipe was known only to her, given to her by her own mother and her mother's mother before her. *Sospiri di monaca*. That's what they were called. The sighs of nuns. Many recipes share this poignant name, but none have ever tasted like the meringues of Paulina's grandmother.

On my seventh birthday, Paulina had taken me by the hand and we had run sweating and serious to her grandmother's bakery, where we both stood silently, looking at the wizened woman. 'Grandmama,' she had said eventually. 'Laura's seven years old today.'

'*E vero?*'

'Yes, it's true.'

With fingers bent and twisted and brown, like an old tree, she put seven 'sighs' in a little basket and handed it to me. I took a meringue and I bit into it. Brittle at first, and then soft, slowly giving up its flavours of golden sugar from the East, roasted hazelnuts from the South and the zest of Tuscan lemons. I closed my eyes. The sigh that came out of my mouth was hot on my hand.

'Oh, sweetheart!' the old woman grinned. 'May all the pleasures in your life be so rapturous and so easy to make.'

In my dreams it's always summer. My mother is still alive, and she's smiling. In the six years since I've been in the convent, slowly but terrifyingly it's dawned on me that I've forgotten the details of her face. It must be because I'm about to be confirmed. They have set the date. I'm to become a Bride of Christ. The older nuns talk about it like a real wedding. An ethereal groom standing stern beside me, looking at me with neither pride nor with lust, but rather with the arrogance of a father, the stillness of a dead saint. The combined power of Doge and Pope.

I wonder if my sister has kept up her drawing. Perhaps she can send me a picture. She was always the better artist, more methodical; I used to become impatient, losing perspective and spoiling the lines with haste.

Mama. Her misty breath, as sweet as sugared almonds, was warm on my skin. I used to breathe her in, that angel mother of mine. I may not be able to see her face any more but I can still smell her: lavender, cinnamon, blossoms of orange and cherry.

My letter is short.

Dear Beatrice,
Please tell me again what Mama's face looked like. Send me a
sketch, if you can.
  Love from your Laura

There's nothing for the Abbess to scratch or blot out. I worry that even the absence of something to censor will somehow frustrate and enrage her.

The Abbess allows the letter to be sent. And then I wait.

2

Three days have passed, and still no letter from Beatrice. The only other letters I receive, perhaps four times a year, are from my brother, Lysander, but he's older than me by ten years – a stranger almost. He lives a scholarly life in Bologna, a place so distant I can't really imagine it. My father never writes at all.

I'm in the convent garden – and so is Abbess Lucrezia. It's too late to turn around. She has seen me seeing her. She fixes her pale, watery old reptilian eyes on me, still and alert.

'You're needed in the infirmary. Go there directly.'

I bow my head and rush off.

It's cool in the infirmary and it smells pleasant today. Candles twinkle and shimmer in the dark. There's a man making a terrible noise – wails and growls like two stray dogs at each other's throats. He's been put on one of the hard infirmary benches. Cushions and blankets are piled around him to protect his thrashing limbs from the bareness of the place. His body twists as though he's possessed. From his mouth comes a whitish yellow froth, like a clump of sea foam left on the Lido on a stormy day. His eyes roll back and the lids quiver.

Sister Maria runs around and around the bench like an ineffectual insect, trying to get near enough to tend to him. She gets close, but one of his limbs lashes out and strikes her, knocking her prayer book out of one hand and a bottle of medicine from the other. She glances at me and runs to the shelf, grabbing a small length of wood.

'He'll bite out his tongue in a moment,' she says. 'Hold his arms!'

I try to restrain his twisting limbs as she attempts to wedge the piece of wood into his mouth. I don't think there's any chance she'll succeed. The man's mouth alternately gapes, wide and drooling, and then clenches shut – immovable and grunting. Sister Maria tries to find an elusive moment in between these contortions to force the wood in between the man's teeth. She gives up the battle and slides away from him, exhausted and sweating, waving an arm limply at me, saying, 'Take over. Take over.'

'What am I to do?'

'Peony root,' she gasps. 'He must swallow the extract from this bottle. If we can't get him to take it, he may die.' She holds the small cracked bottle up in front of me and her hand is trembling so much that some of the liquid comes splashing out. 'And remember – his tongue.' With the other hand she holds up the wooden wedge.

I'm the one who'll have to find a way of getting them into his mouth. I take the bottle and wood and send up a prayer. *Lord give me strength.*

I approach the man very slowly. I touch his chest and feel the power of a stampeding horse rumble inside him. I look straight at his face, and for a second I think that he's looking into my eyes too. But then he rolls and thrashes again and the beast within him seems to swell.

I can do this, I tell myself. I can grapple with fierce things.

Avoiding the worst of his kicking and scratching, I manage to clamber on to him and kneel on his chest. From this height I try to drop the golden peony liquid into his mouth, but his head turns wildly from one direction to another. Sister Maria chants and turns the pages of her book of healing prayer. '*Pray for our sinners now and at the hour of our death. Holy Mary, Mother of God. The Lord is with thee. The Lord is with thee . . .*'

'That's easy for you to say,' I growl quietly as I wrestle with the monster beneath me.

All of a sudden I'm sure there's something wicked about this. I'm squatting on top of a man! I'm touching his body as he writhes and twists beneath me. But Sister Maria doesn't tell me to stop. She carries on chanting in a mournful monotone. I watch the man's face, waiting for the next grotesque, convulsive yawn. My timing is good, because as his mouth opens I clank the lip of the bottle against his teeth and give him some of the medicine. He gags, and I think he's going to choke. I try to put the wooden wedge in then. But gently he splutters it away. The storm is receding.

'*Calma*,' I say quietly to him. '*Calma*.' I touch his hair and wipe his forehead. I'm not sure if I'm supposed to say anything. He shudders like a wild tide going out. Maria doesn't cease her incantations. She's locked into the rhythm of prayer, and seems afraid to stop in case the spell is broken. I don't know if it's the prayer or the peony that's cured him. Perhaps whatever was within him has simply run its course. He stops jerking, and peace ripples through his body. I slide off him, back on to the ground.

The man props himself up on his elbows and looks at me. 'Oh, Christ in heaven, not again. Oh, Jesus, I was near undone.'

'You're much better, sir,' I say to him.

'Yes, well thank you, little sister.' He looks at the bottle of peony oil, almost empty, still in my hand. 'Thank you for taking the poison out of me. I'm almost myself again.'

'Yes, but you're very weak.'

His face darkens and he grabs my arm, pulling me closer to him. 'Weak – what do you mean? How dare you?'

'I'm sorry, sir. I only meant you must be tired. You need rest. You need to drink something.'

He releases me and slumps back on to the bench. 'You're right,' he mutters. 'I'm a weak man. Weak and yielding.'

'Sir, I didn't mean weak of spirit or weak of soul,' I say. 'Just weak in your body. Because of what you've endured.'

He smiles, but his voice is serious. 'No one in Venice can find out what I suffer.'

I promise him I won't tell a soul.

His gaze flickers to Sister Maria. Then he nods, and tells me I'm a good girl. 'I trust you,' he says. 'I do, sincerely.'

Sister Maria ushers me away. She holds a stern finger up to her curled lips: 'Remember, Laura,' she says, 'not a single word about this to anyone. This is a secret. Is that clear? *Uno segreto.*'

I whisper the word to myself a couple of times. It has a dark sound. To say it I have to shut my teeth together and hiss. Then I have to close the back of my throat and roll the tip of my tongue along the roof of my mouth and peep it out between my teeth as if, for a second, that same tongue is trying to escape.

Se − gre − to.

Sibilant at the beginning. Guttural in the middle.

Explosive at the end.

3

At the end of choir practice the next day, I'm filing out of the
chapel when I see Annalena. She's standing at the door and
beckons to me with her finger. She tells me she has a message.
'What? What is it?' I ask as I run along beside her and we wind
our way back to the sleeping quarters.

She refuses to say a thing. 'Wait,' she tells me. 'Will you
wait and stop pestering me?'

Even though I'm superior to her, and she's supposed to do
what I say, every time I look at Annalena I feel envious. There's
something about her that is free and defiant and always
unafraid.

Back in the room she gets me to sit down. She takes off my
veil and tells me my hair is a disgrace. 'Oh, Annalena,' I say to
her, 'is that what you rushed me up here for?'

'No,' she says, and she stands behind me brushing my mop
with long slow strokes. The flimsy curtain hanging over my
window flails like a live, tethered thing in the breeze.
Through that slow flip-flapping, other sounds float up from
the Venetian day: the clicking of heels on stone, the lapping
of water in wind, the shouting of men in boats, the laughter

of children echoing in the side streets around the convent.

Annalena's message is that the Abbess wants to talk to me.

'Really?' I turn to her so that my hair becomes twisted and tangled around the comb.

'Stop that, or the Abbess will make you cut it off.'

'For goodness' sake, Annalena, what does she want to talk to me about?'

'I don't know, but it's something important. I can feel it. Stop thrashing!'

Annalena is clever. Always watching, always noticing. A talent for looking, the Abbess said about her once, although I don't think she meant it as a compliment.

She finishes with the brushing and seems to think me presentable. She says that I'm to go to the Abbess's study straightaway. She tells me not to worry, that God is with me all the time. I look into Annalena's face and she seems so very sad.

My nerves are taut as I make my way to the Abbess's room. Did Sister Maria report the way I behaved in the infirmary with the sick man – the way I climbed on to him? Or has the Abbess intercepted Beatrice's reply? Is there something in it that's put me in terrible trouble?

I remember my father's face on the day he stood outside the great door of this place, giving no salute and showing no emotion as I was dragged in. The flicker of relief in his eyes as I yowled and the nuns prised my fingers from the bars and stepped on my feet to stop me from kicking.

He washed his hands of me that day. My mouth no longer needed to be fed. I was a liability lifted.

I was ten years old, and still didn't understand why it was I and not Beatrice who would be put away. That the dowry is better spent on one good husband than two mediocre ones.

I can still hear his last words before I was pulled through those studded convent doors. 'The fee is paid,' he said to the Abbess.

The fee is never paid. No amount of gold will give me back my joyless days, my listless nights in this prison.

The Abbess motions to me to shut the door. 'Good morning, Sister Laura. Please sit down.'

Any sign of weakness feeds her and makes her even stronger. It's taken me a long time to learn that. I sit, but I manage to hold her watery gaze.

She remains standing. Behind her hangs a great painting from which the rampant lion of the Agliardi Vertova family roars silently down upon the room. Between us, on the table, her Bible sits like a heavy rectangular rock. We all know that the Abbess has a special relationship with God. He comes to her in visions and she translates his lofty words for the rest of us. I think I'm ready for anything. But I'm not prepared for what comes next.

'Laura, you know that I've always counselled the sisters here to learn to expect changes in their lives.'

I've never heard her say this to anyone. Nothing ever changes in the convent.

She continues, solemn, almost reciting, like she's teaching me a new prayer. 'Some changes are great, though at the time they seem small. Others are small, though at the time they seem great.'

She looks crosser and sterner than usual, and I'm sure that Sister Maria has briefed her in clammy detail about my improper conduct in the infirmary. I'm going to spend a year in solitary confinement, where La Lunatica lost her mind. God, don't let her send me there.

The Abbess fingers the golden lettering on her Bible and fondles the silk ribbon bookmark that peeps from the pages in the same way another woman might caress the hand of an infant.

Then she looks up and says: 'You're going to leave the convent, Laura. Someone will be waiting for you at the south entrance at exactly six o'clock.' She doesn't falter and her face is hard like a stone. Nothing except cold, unexplained instruction flickers from her. She hands me a grim little brown bundle wrapped in string. 'These are the clothes you're to wear. We won't see you again.'

For a time I'm completely still. Perhaps it's a cruel game. Or perhaps she's simply testing me.

I don't think there's any wisdom in asking the thousand questions that clatter inside my head. I know that if I do, the Abbess will hold up her smooth pale hand between us. In all the time I've been at the convent, I've never heard her answer a single question. Eventually you learned to stop asking. I suppose that was the idea.

She dismisses me and I walk out to the corridor. La Pungenta is there and she looks at me as though I'm someone she's never seen before.

'What?' I say. 'What have I done?'

'Nothing, Laura. I came looking for you as soon as I heard.'

'Heard what?'

'That you're getting out.'

I feel something waking up inside me. Tonight as the sun goes down on Venice, Beatrice and I will be flying along the pathways and canals as they lap back and forth in celebration beside us. We really will run together to the Lido, and Paulina's grandmother will again give us *sospiri di monaca*, and we will stuff them into our mouths and inhale the sweet powder.

I'll be able to taste again the sugars and spices of this twinkling, shimmering city. Everything is about to change.

4

'La Muta is leaving the convent. She's leaving today! Her father's sent for her.'

I can almost hear them whispering these words even though they don't say anything to me. Somehow I know the news is out. I know from the way that they all turn towards me as I run back to my cell. All these staring women and girls. All their possibilities and dreams and longings emptied out on to the Altar of the Angels, left there the day each was forced to commit herself to Christ.

Happiness can be a cruel thing in the face of someone else's grief. When I tell Annalena, she looks as stricken as if I'd hit her.

'I can't believe it,' she says, her eyes suddenly wet and glassy. 'I'm so happy for you.'

For once, there isn't a hint of mockery in her tone. I clasp her hand then rush back to my room. And as thoughts of Annalena are washed away by the onrushing tide of excitement, I feel guilty. I know already that I won't miss anything about the convent. Not even my *conversa*.

Back in my room, I lift the wooden board that for six years

has hidden my letters from Beatrice, and where I've kept my ring of sisterhood. I open it and take out the tiny cloth-wrapped bundle in which it nests – a dull twist of gold. Beatrice has one too. When Mama realized she was dying, she slid them on to our fingers, murmuring 'You must care for each other when I am gone.' I put the ring back on the small finger of my left hand. For a minute it feels cold and tight. But then it warms and settles back into place, where it belongs.

As I pass back through the convent, plumes of incense waft behind me for the last time. Mounds of chapel wax drip like tears as I say my final prayers. And the pungent baskets in the infirmary, full of holy herbs, creak a brittle farewell to me.

At six o'clock the carriage really is waiting. Sister Maria stands at the door and kisses me.

'Goodbye, Laura. I'll miss you. We all will.'

It feels like someone is pouring something warm into me. The convent's dark, cold skin peels away as soon as I run out through the thick studded door. I dive into the carriage almost headfirst.

The carriage is black and the driver wears a dark hat and coat, but everything else out here is a banquet of colour: red, gold, blue, leaf green. I look up to the windows of the convent's cells. The silhouette of a nun hovers at almost every one of those small rectangular spaces. There's a shadow in Annalena's window, but I'm not sure it's her.

Venice throngs with the festival of the Madonna delle Candele. Smells of perfume and aromatic oils mingle with other things – sulphur, I think, and ripe fruit. Each moment takes me further away from the convent and closer to my home. I lean out of the carriage window and see serpentine lanes of small candles, spitting with spray from the canals. But as I twist round my elbow whacks into a young man on a milk cart.

'Oh, sir, I'm so terribly sorry,' I shout, feeling my cheeks flush.

The young man smiles, calling back, 'No need to be sorry! Always a pleasure to collide with a beautiful girl.'

The carriage crosses the rickety old Rialto Bridge with its orchestra of sounds and smells. This is what it must feel like to be drunk.

When we come to a halt, I fall forward. I'm home.

It's strange to be back at this once-shimmering palazzo of my childhood. When I was little, I peeped out of my bedroom window and I would see servants and noblemen, old and young, rich and poor – all hurrying along. But they would always pause to look up at my home and almost all of them would smile, as if the very building were casting a spell of pleasure on them all. My home used to sparkle and glitter.

It doesn't any more.

The plaster has shrunk and peeled from the walls like mouldy orange peel, and damp stains streak beneath the shutters on the upper floors. The plants and flowers in the window boxes are dying.

The great front door is open and I walk in, my footfall echoing on the cracked marble floor. The cool of the house slips its embrace around me. Where once portraits hung on the walls, now there are empty, pale spaces.

'Beatrice?' I call. There's no answer.

Something large and dark has been placed on the table in the entrance hall. It takes me a few minutes to realize that it's a coffin.

My father walks through a side door that I remember leads from his library. If the house has suffered, then he has wilted with it. His clothes were made for a bigger, broader man. They drape over him like threadbare blankets.

'Papa.' I hold one hand out to him as he approaches, but he doesn't take it. There's something new and grim about his face.

'Papa, who is it? Who's died?'

He swallows hard, as if his words are caught in his throat.

It must be one of the servants. A lot of them were old. Renato, my father's butler, was an alcoholic. And then I think of my beloved nurse, Faustina, and my mind fills up with images of her kind old face.

'Tell me, Papa, that it isn't Faustina.' I shake my head and step away from him.

When he finally speaks, his voice is solemn, hoarse and faintly slurred.

'It's not Faustina.'

My poor brother, then. He never was a strong boy. Perhaps he contracted some illness in Bologna. Almost as soon as the thought occurs, I realize my mind is performing logical contortions to avoid the truth. If he died so far south of Venice, they wouldn't bring him all the way here.

So before I even see who is lying still and silent in the coffin, I already know that this is somehow not the wonderful day I thought it was going to be. I'm not going to see Beatrice today. I'm not going to see her ever again.

I open my mouth but no sound comes out. My father shields his face with a hand.

I reach the edge of the wooden box. My sister's hands are yellow and bloated. Her face sags and suddenly it's hard to remember any of the light that once danced in it. Her body is small but swollen and it looks dreadfully wrong inside that cheap container for dead things. The exquisite mystery of her is gone.

The unsanded wood scratches my arms and hands as my father drags me away from the coffin, but I don't care. I want the splintered wood to stick into me. I want to feel the rough slivers under my skin.

'What did you expect?' he asks. 'Why did you think I sent for you? Did the Abbess not explain?'

She did not.

Beatrice died by drowning, my father tells me. I can't speak. I can't ask the questions that bang like demented drums in my temples. How could she have drowned? Where did she drown? And why? Beatrice, the best swimmer in all of Venice. She used to dart through the water, strong and shiny like a seal.

I push my father away and rush up the stairs to the room I shared with Beatrice. A hunched figure is standing over the bed, unfolding a linen sheet. She turns to me.

Faustina.

'Oh, my darling,' she says, dropping everything and opening her arms.

After a time, we sit beside each other on the bed and talk. We speak of how we've missed each other. Of how I've grown and changed. I say she doesn't look any different, but she does.

I was wrong about everything. I thought I was coming home to Beatrice, but I was not. I did not think I was going to miss Annalena at all, but I do.

I feel that the dark serpent of loss has crawled inside my body; it lurks there, coiled and muscular. I do not think it will ever leave.

5

I'm woken by a slant of sunlight blazing across my pillow. The sun seems to bleed through the cracks in the window shutters, like some ancient injured enemy who wishes to punish me for something that I haven't done.

I sit opposite my father as we eat a breakfast of bread and cured meats. Bianca, a servant I haven't met before, waits on us, filling our goblets with pomegranate juice and slicing oily ribbons from the leg of ham that rests at the centre of the table. Her head is bowed and respectful, but I can see her blue eyes darting curiously between my father's face and my own. I wonder if she's also trying to recognize the proud man he used to be. Now he's broken and bent and he speaks in a low mumble that I have to lean forward to hear.

'You and I will have to find a way through this dreadful situation.'

I reach across the table for his hand and he strokes my fingers gently, absentmindedly, with his thumb – he's somewhere else. When I speak, he almost looks surprised to see me.

'Papa, I'm lost. Lost without Beatrice.'

'I know, Laura, but there's much to do. Trust me. You will

be happy again. It may seem impossible, but you will recover, and we will be strong once more.'

I shake my head, unable to believe his words. 'Not without Beatrice.'

He sits up, and looks sternly at me, as if I'm a whingeing child who needs to be spoken to more firmly.

'You behaved exactly like this after your mother died. It wasn't helpful then.'

'No, but . . .'

'Time heals. And it will heal now, just as it did then.'

I let go of my father's hand and he slumps a little. I tear off a strip of bread, staring at my chipped plate as I swallow down a hot rush of tears. Time doesn't heal; it destroys. The brightness playing through the windows shifts. I blink, dazzled, and for a moment the trembling light makes it seem that my mother is sitting with us.

In a rush it comes back to me – her face as clear as it ever was. I remember how she once sat on my bed in the middle of a winter night, stroking my damp hair, my five-year-old face wet and frightened after a dark nightmare.

'Mama, will the snakes come and get me in my sleep?'

'Hush, my angel, hush, there are no snakes. Go back to sleep.'

'But what if I dream of them again?'

'Next time, don't wake up until the dream is over. If you see it through, you'll find that everything is all right in the end. Nothing bad will ever touch you.'

Mama, you were wrong too.

While Bianca clears the plates, I add this to the list of things I know for sure.

The fee is never paid.

Time destroys.

Nothing will be all right.

I'm building my personal catechism. I'm committing it to memory, these ugly lessons that life is teaching me.

I excuse myself from the table and step out into the bitter morning glow of the courtyard at the rear of the house. I walk over the flagstones and lean against the wrought-iron back gate, which leads to a narrow waterway. Thousands of tiny pieces of dust are turning in the sunlight, floating and falling around me: a lifeless dance of decay.

Later, I sit on the floor in the dressing chamber I shared with Beatrice, a linen chest open in front of me, and begin the sad task of sorting her clothes. My father has said that I am already taller than my sister was; since I can't wear her garments, they must be discarded. Gently I take out her stays, her shawls and underskirts, and lay them in piles. Some will be sold, others cut up and sewn into something new.

Faustina comes in, a stool in her gnarled hands. 'Sit here, my love,' she says, putting it beside me. 'The floor's no place for a lady.'

She gently takes a silken headdress from me as I move, then opens the tall, dark wooden cupboard that contains Beatrice's gowns. As she folds rich velvet and soft satin, I ask her questions as they come to me.

'How did Beatrice drown? Where were you?'

'Stop, Laura, please stop,' she says. 'Please don't keep asking me. I can't.'

But I have to know and gradually she tells me. Beatrice and

Faustina had been to the concert at the Palazzo. Beatrice's dancing feet quick-stepped home, the way I always picture her
flitting around the courtyard.

'Faustina, was she with you? Was she beside you when she
fell in?'

'Yes. I mean no. We *were* together, but . . .' she replies, fumbling
and dropping a blue gown. It lands in a collapsed heap, its empty
bodice gaping wide. 'Beatrice wanted to talk to someone she
knew. You remember what she was like, chatting and laughing
with every second person she met – day or night, she was the
same. She told me to walk on ahead – that she'd return once she'd
paid a visit to his friend. She knew I can't move quickly any more,
and that I was tired and in a hurry to get home.'

Faustina sighs. She picks up the fallen gown, placing it on
a dressing table, then puts her old arms around me. She
murmurs that she wishes she could make everything better the
way she always could when I was small and when the troubles
I had were solved by a kiss and a pastry from the kitchen. But
my mind is still on the night Beatrice died.

'Do you think she went to see Vincenzo?' I ask, thinking
of her fiancé.

But Faustina shudders and holds her knotted hands up in
front of her face.

I hear my father's heavy footfall and he pushes open the
door, his faded cloak flapping. His eyes are bright, his stance
no longer defeated but upright and purposeful.

'The time for crying is over, Laura. There's life to live and
business to attend to. You have responsibilities now – and a
duty to ensure the dignity of our family.'

He offers me his hand. I take it and he leads me from the room. Faustina's fingers clutch at mine as we pass, her eyes dimmed with sadness. Dread twists in my stomach. What is it she fears?

I look at my father's profile as we go downstairs. He catches my eye as we reach the hall.

'Don't look so worried. It's good news. And besides, it will take your mind off our loss.'

He brings me to the courtyard where we sit near the outstretched branch of the cypress tree. An arm's length above us, it has hundreds of tiny glistening insects crawling in and out of its crevices.

'You know that Vincenzo was an excellent match for your sister,' says my father. 'You know that they were to be wed in the spring?'

I did know that, of course, but I had heard almost nothing else of Beatrice's betrothed. For a moment I see the Abbess's face glowing in the light of the holy candle flame with which she burned sinful letters, eliminating the impure thoughts contained in dangerous ink. Maybe my sister's thoughts about Vincenzo never reached me. Perhaps he's handsome and smiling. Maybe there were burned letters that talked about Vincenzo's love for her, and hers for him, and other things they might have whispered secretly to each other.

'He'll be devastated,' I said.

'Upset, yes. But this is not an irretrievable situation.'

His words, so oddly business-like, make me stiffen.

'How can it possibly be remedied?' I ask, staring at my father. 'There can be no wedding without a bride.'

Dark lines thicken on his brow.

'Of course there will be a wedding,' he scoffs. 'Why else do you think you're here?'

6

I may as well be La Muta again. I can say nothing.

'Cousins of the Doge will be there!' my father says. 'No less than seven members of the Grand Council have already accepted invitations. There's still a chance we may even be honoured by the Doge himself because of Vincenzo's connections. How can we possibly turn down such an opportunity?'

The evening is warm and when I go up to my bedroom without dinner Faustina is there, opening my window. The flames of a citronella candle jerk inside a little coloured pot beside my bed. It's supposed to keep the insects away but it's not doing any good tonight. A mosquito drones and buzzes somewhere nearby.

With a sharp 'Hah!' Faustina claps her palms together, declaring victory.

'I don't have to do what Father asks, do I?' I say, slipping into bed. Faustina smoothes out the cool sheet over my body then sits beside me, stroking my forehead.

'Darling, we must do what we are told. It's better for us in the long run. Men are the rulers of the world.'

It might be one more thing I need to add to my catechism. She's right, I know. *Even in the convent*, I think. *Even in a world where no men set foot*. I remember how my father spoke to me in the courtyard, the way he beckoned me with that small flick of his fingers back into the parlour.

I touch Faustina's rough hand. 'What's Vincenzo like?'

'Oh, my darling,' she says, 'I really cannot tell you. I've seen so little of him. He rarely came here, and when he did, it was only to talk business with your father in his library.'

'Is he handsome?'

The bed ripples as Faustina shifts, turning towards the open window. 'He's a member of the Council,' she says. 'Tall, with good bearing and a fine lineage.'

'But what if I don't like him?'

When she faces me again, there are big tears quivering in her eyes. She brushes them away with her wrinkled hands.

'Shush, darling. It's so much better for you to be married. At least you'll be out here in the city, and not locked away where we can never see you! And old Faustina will always be here for you. I promise you that.' She smiles, though tears fall freely over her cheeks. 'I'll miss having you here, that's all. But soon you'll be a grand woman with a home of your own, children will arrive, and your worries will be few.'

She begins to hum. I've known this tune for a long, long time. She sang it to Beatrice and I when we were tiny, and when we grew older we sang it to each other. *Stellina, stellina, bella stellina*. Beautiful little star. For a little while, those words sound like the beating of my own heart.

As night draws over the sky, I can't sleep. Slipping on a robe,

I go out into the garden. There I spend an hour gathering Beatrice's favourite flowers by lantern-light. The smell of the lavender is strong enough to make me feel dizzy. I pick the blossoms of nutty gorse and pull the powdery wild roses away from the garden's tangled bushes. I carry my hoard indoors and arrange the flowers around Beatrice's body so that she's nestled in a haze of fragrant greens and purples and blues and pinks.

I imagine what it will be like to meet Vincenzo and to talk to him. He might help me to stay close to her – to keep that memory alive. *He is a perfect match for me*, she said in one of her letters. In another she talked about how her marrying him would serve us all well. And I do remember her saying that he was kind and good. At least, I *think* I remember her telling me that.

I weave a crown of white blossoms into her golden hair. But the luminous petals make her look even emptier, and now that I've torn them from their natural places, they have started to die too. What did I think? That framing her face with flowers would bring her back to life? Her body is a broken instrument and it's never going to sing again.

I kiss her chilly forehead. There's a stack of wood by the sooty grate, and I build a fire. I stand beside the coffin, gazing at her waxy face.

'Beatrice, remember when I got stuck at the top of the cypress tree in the courtyard? I jumped and you caught me. You rolled us over and you tickled me and we laughed so hard that tears fell from our eyes.' I hold her limp hand in my own and laugh at the memory of it, amazed that my body is still able to form such a sound.

And that is when I see something strange. My disconcertion

condenses into fright, like warm breath meeting the cold of a windowpane. There is a pale mark on her finger, in the place where her ring of sisterhood should be.

A coldness rushes through me. I look at my own ring of twisted gold and Beatrice's handwriting seems to appear in front of my eyes: '*I wear our ring of sisterhood. I'll never take it off . . .*'

Faustina pads across the hallway holding out a plate of peaches on a silver tray. She tells me I must eat, and scolds me for being thin.

'Faustina. Where is Beatrice's ring?'

She sets the tray down on a low table beside the door and moves closer to me. 'What ring, love?'

'The ring she always wore. You know? Exactly the same as this one.' I hold my hand up in front of my face like a fan. 'Did she have it on the day she died? Was she wearing it?'

'Darling, I can't remember. There was so much happening, I –'

'Someone must have taken it,' I say.

Faustina takes my arm and leads me away from Beatrice. Her movements are slow and weary. 'There's nothing we can do about any of this now, little one. Please try not to get so upset. It's not going to bring her back to us.'

But my head is thumping, and I feel something new inside me getting swollen and sore like a boil. Who was it that took my sister's ring?

Faustina picks up the tray of peaches and she ushers me back up the stairs. 'Come, child. Eat. For me.'

The peach tastes bitter. I spit it out into my hand.

7

'*Stellina, Stellina. Bella Stellina!*'

Beatrice's voice wafts into my bedroom. It brings our old song floating on the morning. I throw the covers off my bed and pad over to my door, along the corridor and up the stairs towards that hopeful and happy sound. For some reason she's in the servants' quarters, on the upper floors of the palazzo.

She's come back to me. All is not lost!

The voice becomes clearer and cleaner. My loneliness for her starts to peel away as my bare feet rush across the cold marble. The first of the upper chambers is locked. I slap my hand against the door with a growl, then run to the next room. The handle turns. I burst inside to find Faustina folding sheets. Her gentle old face is startled.

'Sweetheart!' she says. 'What on earth are you doing?'

But I turn and rush from the room. I'll find her. I know she's here somewhere waiting for me. The song gets louder. I stumble as I race back to the landing and up the final set of stairs – the highest in the palazzo. At the top is a small chamber that used to be my mother's sewing room.

This is where the sound is coming from. I open the door.

It's Bianca.

As she sings, she stitches the seam of a red velvet dress, expensive and luscious, embroidered on its breast with a lattice of jewels. It's so rich and deep in colour and its beads and stones are so dazzling that the sight of it shatters my desperate fantasy. Beatrice isn't singing; Beatrice is dead.

I slide to the floor, panting for breath.

Bianca jumps up. 'Ma'am! I didn't realize . . .' She rummages among the baskets of fabric and thread and pulls out a handkerchief, its borders embroidered with an orange blossom pattern. She hands it to me and I press the pretty cloth to my damp face.

When my breathing has slowed I smile at her. 'You have a beautiful voice,' I tell her. 'How do you know that song?'

Her face softens. 'Your sister taught it to me.'

I hear Faustina's slow footfall on the stairs. Bianca takes my hand and pulls me upright, as I steady myself against the collapse of my foolish hope.

Faustina rounds the doorway, her brow drawn in concern. But she smiles when she sees the red dress and hobbles forward to stroke its soft folds. 'Bianca, this is wonderful – it's almost ready!'

'Ready for what?' I ask.

Faustina's eyes twinkle. 'For you, my love. You're to wear it tonight – when you meet Vincenzo.'

I haven't been able to eat. I can't relax. A party, Faustina tells me. A gathering of the nobles of Venice at the Doge's palace. I've spent the morning drifting around the courtyard, imagining what this evening will be like and trying to comprehend that I am to go to a party, while my sister's body lies still and cold.

Our midday meal is over. Faustina, Bianca and I cluster in my room. They wash and dress me, but it's nothing like the cold baths at the convent. Everything feels heavy with expectation: the splashing of the water; the mixing of the oils; the drying of my body; the dabbing of the scents. The whispering of the rich deep red dress Bianca brings down from the sewing room. It swishes along the floor, rustling conspiratorially – ribbons, silk, velvet and satin. Bianca lowers it over my head. An intense silence settles. Faustina has told me that they have been instructed to create a masterpiece. She stands behind me, drawing tight the laces of the bodice while Bianca adjusts the neckline. Her face is solemn and focused on the challenge.

My dress fastened, Bianca brushes my hair until the tresses are completely free of knots. Annalena would be proud. Faustina cleans and shapes my fingernails and rubs a tiny drop of olive oil into my palms to soften them. Bianca murmurs for me to lower my head, and fixes two bone combs, embedded with precious gems, into my hair.

They stand back to study their work. Bianca nods approvingly and Faustina pushes me gently into the anteroom, standing me before the mirror.

'Look at you,' she whispers.

I've spent years in shabby brown and black and grey, my hair hidden under a headdress, my hands rough with work. Now I'm looking into a dream. The girl reflected in it is nothing like me at all. She never appeared in my secret shard of mirror at the convent. My hair is so shiny that it almost glistens. My nails are white. I'm smooth and sparkling. I can't stop looking at myself and feel a crinkle of excitement shudder through me.

Faustina holds me by the shoulders, looking at the mirror with her old cheek pressed against mine. 'Sweetheart, you're perfect.'

Bianca doesn't agree. 'Hmmm,' she says, frowning. 'Almost, but not quite. I know what should be the finishing touch.'

She rushes from the room, returning with a dark wooden box that I recognize. It's where my mother's jewels are kept.

'No!' Faustina shouts at Bianca, and she hurries over, trying to pull the box from her hands. 'You don't have permission.'

Bianca holds the box high, out of Faustina's reach. 'Oh, for goodness' sake, her day is here: she should have the rubies. They'll be perfect with the dress. She'll look like royalty and her father will be so pleased.'

'Bianca, do *not* open that box,' Faustina says. There's a strange tone to her voice – not authority or annoyance, but panic.

Bianca whirls away, laughing, from Faustina's clutching hands. She holds the box in front of me, quickly flipping the hinged lid over. Her smile turns to dismay.

There's nothing in there at all. Not a single ruby. Not a stone.

'They're *gone*!' shouts Bianca. She tosses the empty box aside and it clatters on the marble floor. 'We must tell Signor della Scala. There's been a robbery!'

With a sigh, Faustina runs her fingers through her grey hair. She sits heavily on the bed, her shoulders slumped.

'No, there has not been a robbery,' she says firmly.

I sweep my skirts over my arm and stoop down to rescue the box. Closing the lid, I hand it to my nurse. I know something is wrong.

'Faustina,' I ask. 'What happened to my mother's jewels?'

'Your father sold them,' she said. 'His income is not what it was. I had hoped . . .' and she glares at Bianca, 'to explain it to you more gently.'

Faustina sends her to see that the barge will be ready to take me to the party. I sit on the bed and Faustina tells me that my father has been stripping the palazzo of its treasures. This is what the empty spaces on the walls mean. I don't really care. The greatest treasure is lost to me already, her body lying in her coffin.

The barge awaits. Bianca walks beside me to the door, beaming.

'Are you excited about seeing the Doge, ma'am?' she asks.

I cling to the stone banister as I move down the wide, curved staircase, fearful that I might trip over the folds of red fabric and tumble down to the marble floor.

'Are you?' Bianca insists. There is a tinge of sadness in her voice, and I realize that many girls in this city would envy me tonight.

I squeeze Bianca's hand. 'If I meet him I'll tell you every detail.'

My father emerges from his library, looking twice his normal size in fine hose and great padded shoulders of tan velvet. When he sees me, he smiles and his face softens.

'My sweet Laura,' he says, and I blush at the unfamiliar praise. 'How wonderful. You're just the thing.'

He takes my arm and we step out into Venice.

8

As the carriage clatters along the cobbles, my father pats my hand and tells me what I'm to do and how I'm to behave at the Doge's palace.

'Vincenzo will be the centre of attention, of course, and so will several members of the Grand Council.' He leans forward to brush an invisible speck of something or other off my cape. 'Remember, Laura, that you're not a child any more. You're on show this evening. Our future depends on it.'

At the edge of the Grand Canal we step out of the carriage and on to the barge. My heavy skirts mean that one of the young bargemen has to lift me over the side. His hands around my waist are broad and flat, almost like the oar that rests dripping over the water. He smiles as he places me on the deck, but quickly looks away as my father clambers on board and sits at the prow, his pale hands and his wrists folded in front of him.

I take my place beside him and the great whale of a boat lumbers towards St Mark's Square. We pass the Rialto – that arch of dark wood linking the east side of the city to the west – and into more open water. My father doesn't seem to notice, but I can feel it: the chill of my sister's last moments. Where did she fall? It was somewhere near here. I lean out a little and look down into the water – that inky liquid grave.

We pass the sparkling buildings and lights of Venice. The great tall houses cast their stretched reflections on to the water, where they mingle with that of the moon. Distant laughter bounces off the hard surfaces of stone.

My father's expression is taut in the succession of shadow and light, and I realize that his face is powdered, to smooth the tired lines. I wonder if he is worrying about the impression I will make. There will be things he'll want me to do and to say – rules I don't know and rituals I've never had a hand in, patterns of talk that I've never been part of. I'm able to chant glories to God for hours. I can force oil of peony root into the mouth of a crazed man, breaking him like some restless colt. I can sit silent and still for hours in a cell, pretending to be at prayer. But I don't know anything about parties.

The air seems to thicken as we get closer. I sit with my fists closed and my elbows pressed hard into my ribs, and my father laughs.

'Not so tense,' he says gently. 'Not so rigid, Laura.' I laugh at myself too, and then he points and says, 'Look!'

I see the palace like something rising out of the water. White and gold. Arches on arches, all flickering with the lights of the party. Other boats are converging, drifting near the jetty to deposit their flamboyant cargo. Already I hear a hum of conversation coming from within the walls. And there's music. Lutes, bells, flutes and harpsichord all tangled together.

Nothing like the solemn purity of our songs inside the convent. Our turn arrives and the bargeman steers us expertly alongside the alighting point. The music makes my body move. I'm intoxicated already.

'It's beautiful!' I say.

'Yes, it is,' my father replies.

A lush crowd throngs at the entrance to the palace. People dart jovial *hellos* and *how-are-yous* at each other. As well as the palace, the guests are shimmering too. Beautiful, coloured, bejewelled. Footmen and maids weave between them, carrying scarves and capes and veils.

Stepping on to solid ground, and up the steps, my silken petticoats rustle along the stone. I shiver slightly as we pass into the shadow of the entrance.

Two footmen open the vast double doors for us and we walk into a great hallway. The walls are glowing marble and the ceiling frescoed with laughing cherubs. In the centre is a statue of a nymph, her hands clasped to her breast. I whirl around, seeing myself in every polished surface. Except it's not me. I'm tall and poised and graceful. When I see my reflection on the wall my dress seems to be a ruby jewel, as bright as the missing gems of my mother. Other people are looking at me in a way that makes me want to smile. Their eyes rest a fraction too long, or their brows shift upwards as though I'm a long-forgotten friend now returned.

There's a rumble of voices ahead and we walk through a sparkling encrusted doorway into the ballroom. Gilded mirrors and candelabras hang from the walls, the hundreds of candles sparking pins of light that dance and tumble around like fireworks. A lute quartet plays a lively dance, the notes hanging among the chatter. I hold my father's hand tightly as we move through the other guests. Glorious-looking women and handsome men enter the ballroom together, and then slowly drift apart. The men smile at me with eyes as sharp as arrows. I let my own eyes meet some of the more brazen stares, and I see these people aren't all as beautiful as distance makes them. Complexions are powdered, flesh shows crinkles of laughter around the eyes and lips. Men with broad shoulders and red cheeks stand in leather shoes that shine so brightly they look wet. Gleaming buckles flash in the light. The women tilt their lace fans, silken gowns shimmering. Perfume hangs heavy in the air. But among the joyful crowd are those who seem apart from the scene; they chatter and flirt, but their eyes are hollow with hunger and desperation.

'I refuse to pay a gondolier ever again,' a woman in a blue dress complains. 'I prefer to walk until the soles of my shoes wear out.'

'You need to be a criminal to survive,' says her companion, flicking her fan in annoyance. 'Those wretched Turkish wars have ruined everything for the honest businessman.'

Great bursts of laughter ring out from time to time, as if they have been planned ahead – as if there's some hidden conductor of mirth directing these eruptions of studied delight. I've heard these sounds before. They're the echoes of my childhood – the noise of the glamorous, the privileged, the powerful – the tinkle and the clash of the rich.

My father nudges me towards the two women. 'Say hello. Head up. Smile.' When I do, they dip their heads and curtsy.

My father bows to them and we move on to the next cluster of guests. 'You're causing quite a stir! Keep it up,' he says.

I'm not exactly sure what he's praising, but somehow I don't even have to try to be sociable. There is a festive air that makes me want to smile and nod and greet people. Some of the men run their eyes down me as though there's a message scrawled from the top of my head to the tips of my shoes and they're trying to read it. I imagine the Abbess's disapproving stare and tingle with pleasure.

A tall woman in a silvery dress stands talking to a large group. Her hair is coiled around her head, its grey streaks gleaming like the steely fabric of her gown. The skin on her face and neck is etched with delicate lines, but it's as clear and soft as a young girl's. And although she laughs and chatters with her companions, her green eyes are fixed on me.

I dip my head in greeting and she smiles, a mixture of bemusement and approval. I smile back, and she takes this as a signal, excusing herself and moving through the other guests towards me. My composure leaves me at once. I look to my father, but suddenly he is no longer at my side and I turn to see him with a group of men. What should I do? I'm not ready to —

'Hello, Laura,' says the woman, her voice clear and deep. She takes my hand, her movements graceful. I wonder how she knows my name.

'I'm Allegreza di Rocco. And you, Laura, are a della Scala are you not? Poor Beatrice's sister.'

'Yes,' I say. 'I am — I mean I was. I mean I always will be.' A surge of blood sets fire to my cheek.

'You're quite right.' Allegreza's elegant face softens. 'Alive or dead, once a sister, always a sister.'

An old woman steps close to her, her face pinched with worry. She mutters quietly to Allegreza, who nods.

'Excuse me, Laura. We will talk again – soon,' she says. She puts her arm around the old woman and gently manoeuvres her away.

I stand alone for a moment. This woman, Allegreza; she knew me. Or of me, at least. But what does she wish to speak to me about? Surely a girl just released from a convent couldn't be of interest to her.

'Madam?' A servant with a tray of glasses appears at my side.

I take one, cradling it carefully so as not to spill the clear golden liquid. I hear my father shout with laughter. He's still huddled with other men at the far side of the ballroom, and the task of reaching him, of negotiating the other guests without being detained, seems as impossible as crossing the Hellespont on foot; I might be caught up in the undercurrents of innuendo, or dashed on the rocks of jokes I can't understand. So I stay where I am, and take a sip of wine. It tastes of syrup and summer, and after the plain water of the convent, like ambrosia slipping down my throat. Almost immediately, the sweetness seems to rush to my head. Annalena once told me the Abbess kept a bottle of wine, fermented by the monks on the island of San Michele, in her chamber; she'd disturbed her once and heard the bottle clinking as the Abbess hurriedly hid it away. I can't believe it was true, for how could her face always have been so sour?

The musicians lower their instruments and the room hushes. One by one, I notice the heads of the guests turning in the direction of the main doors, their faces concerned. A couple around the same age as my father stand there – both handsome, upright, solemn. Their clothes are black, and among the gaudy costumes and luxurious materials of the revellers, seem like some sort of reproach. The man looks straight ahead while holding his wife's arm firmly, like someone holding a tiller to steer a boat. Her eyes are to the floor, and she's rubbing the beads of a black rosary between her long white fingers. They walk slowly but deliberately through the guests.

'Is that who I think it is?' I hear a man hiss behind me.

'They shouldn't have come,' says a rotund woman in a green silk gown.

The crowd parts at the far side of the ballroom and I see another figure making his way towards the new arrivals. I only glimpse his profile and then his back. His doublet is purple and edged with gold, and the ruff around his neck is very white. Two guards follow close behind, swords hanging at their sides.

'The Doge is going to speak to them!' says the woman.

The Doge? I remember Bianca's excitement. Now that I'm in the same room as the most powerful man in Venice, curiosity burns inside me. The other guests move towards him, jostling to see what will happen next. This room of well-heeled socialites exchanging pleasantries is undergoing a strange metamorphosis: the transformation is an unpleasant one. Or perhaps it was always like this: not a group of civilized citizens, but a reeking mob. It makes my blood quicken.

I slide as close to the front as I can, standing on tiptoes to see over the wigs and headdresses, my balance supported by the press of the crowd.

The Doge stops in front of the black-clad couple. They face him with hard, sad faces. Who are they? Why would they challenge the most powerful man in Venice? The Doge shakes his head, then turns to the guards behind him.

It cannot be.

With that first view of his face comes the realization that I've seen this man, the Doge, before. I want to hide, but there's nowhere to go. I've felt breath from his nostrils on my skin. I've held his arms and struggled with him like we were wrestlers, or animals.

The Doge of Venice is the crazed man from the convent. And, in this room, only I know his secret.

9

The Doge beckons his guards towards the couple.

'Turn around and leave by the doors through which you've entered,' he orders.

If his words are meant to intimidate, they only half succeed. The woman's face trembles, but the man stands straighter still.

'We have as much a right to be here as any of the families of the province,' he says. 'Asserting that right is what we have come to do.'

A gasp ripples across the room.

'You have no rights to be asserted,' says the Doge. 'This is a private gathering and you have not been invited. How dare you come here?'

They don't have the chance to answer him. He raises his arm, strong and firm – that very same arm that I held to stop it thrashing and flailing. The guards seize the couple, dragging them towards the door. The woman screams and the man bellows, 'You will not insult the name of my family. The de Ferraras will not be humiliated.'

'Stop. Enough, Julius,' his wife says. Her face twists with some inner pain.

The guards release them and they walk together towards the door. The woman tries to take her husband by the arm but he shrugs her off.

The doors clang shut. The moment is over, and the music begins once more. The Doge moves back among the crowd, his power exercised, and a retinue of male guests follow, their faces grim. I pray he won't come this way. I was wearing my habit the last time we met, and he was in a daze when we spoke, but still, he looked right at me. '*I'm a weak man. Weak and yielding. No one in Venice can find out what I suffer.*' His words that day in the convent make a new kind of sense to me. If Venice knew what I know, would its people still grant him such loyalty?

My thoughts must be playing across my face, as the woman with the green dress I saw earlier takes my arm and pulls me into her circle.

'Oh, my dear, don't look so startled!' she says.

I smile gratefully.

'Do you know what that was about?' a woman with feathers in her hair asks, her eyebrows raised.

'No,' I say, 'I've no idea.'

The women laugh, delighted, I guess, to have an ingénue to tutor.

'That was the de Ferraras – Julius and Grazia,' says the woman in green. 'They have a feud with the Doge and his family.' She pats my arm playfully. 'How could you live in Venice and not know that?'

'I've been . . . absent,' I say.

'Perhaps you were too young when it all started. It must

have been ten years ago now. The Doge executed the de Ferraras' only son, Carlo, when he was just a young lawyer,' she continues. 'On charges of conspiracy, apparently.' She stops to cross herself, her plump hand moving rapidly across her bosom.

The woman wearing the feathers continues. 'Julius took the only revenge he could. His men killed Roberto – the Doge's son. So tall and handsome that boy was. Only eleven.'

Her eyes glisten as she speaks, but not with tears. They brim with histories, backgrounds, stories, reasons, accounts of old scores.

'Oh yes, such an awful business that was!' exclaims the woman in the green gown. 'The noblest among us are always those in most danger, isn't that what they say?' The women nod, and she sighs. 'But young men are such a worry. So full of passion and principle.'

'I always advise my boy not to take life so seriously,' says another. 'Take things with a pinch of salt, that's what I say. I mean, goodness, we have quite enough to worry about, what with the Turks and pirates ruining my husband's business. Honestly, I can't keep my daughters in silk these days.'

They laugh. The big woman drips with gold, her green dress stretched over her vast bosom like a yawn of satin. I wish that Annalena could see, or that I could tell her everything. I want to sit in the window of our cell with the white curtain dancing in the breeze and see her eyes widen.

Their laughter fades as they stare behind me. I turn to a handsome equerry, dressed in a livery of grey and red. Beside him is the Doge and a finely dressed woman I guess must be the Doge's wife. Jewels glitter from her ears and about her neck.

The equerry indicates me with a flourish and I step forward. 'Your Grace,' he says to the Doge, 'may I present Laura, Antonio della Scala's youngest.'

'Ah yes,' the Doge says. He looks straight at me.

My breathing has lost its rhythm, and I stammer as I drop into a clumsy curtsy. 'Your Grace.'

There isn't the slightest glimmer of recognition in his eyes. His wife regards me with a quizzical smile.

'Make sure Vincenzo treats you properly,' she says to me.

They move on past to other people, all hungry for a kiss of the Doge's ring, a shake of his hand or a single word from the most powerful man in Venice.

I step out of the path of a dancing couple, too wrapped up in each other's gaze to notice me. The girl's skirts brush mine as they whip past. Across the ballroom couples spiral and turn in time to the music. I'm amazed by the way hands openly rest upon bodies, cheeks press against cheeks.

A young woman with a bright face rushes across the room, skipping through the dancers. There's something familiar about her: very pretty, high cheekbones, a slender neck. Her dress is cream, dotted with crystals, and her shoulders bare but for her tumbling black curls. The remembered taste of meringues sits on my tongue. I *do* know her – and her grandmama, with her *sospiri di monaca*. The last time I saw Paulina she was softer and rounder. An apple-cheeked little girl has been replaced by this grown-up and willowy woman.

'Hello, hello, sweet Laura!' she says, kissing me quickly, once on each cheek. She hugs me close and I want to laugh and then I want to cry. Because she was, she *is*, my friend.

'How many years?' she asks. 'How many since I last saw you? Four?'

'Six,' I say. 'You look beautiful!'

'Not as beautiful as you!' she says. 'You know that all the men are talking about you already. Have you been flirting?'

I blush. 'I . . .'

'I see,' laughs Paulina, and she wags a finger playfully at my cheeks. 'You can even bring rose blossoms to your face at will. Just like your sister.' The words fall from her mouth, and seem to drop to the ground as heavily as the statue in the hallway. Her smile vanishes. 'I'm so sorry.'

'That's all right,' I say quickly, desperately wanting to change the subject. 'How are you? How's your grandmama?'

'Oh, she died three years ago!' says Paulina. 'I wrote to tell you, but you never replied. We all thought that you'd turned to God, after all.'

I remember the Abbess, holding sheets of parchment over a candle. Paulina's letter would have been among them.

'I wrote to you all the time,' I say. 'For the first couple of years. Sometimes every day. The censors were strict, though.'

Paulina squeezes my hand.

'Are you married?' I ask.

Paulina gives me a sly grin. 'Not yet.' She lowers her voice. 'I can't tell you about it here – but I will. Now, what was it like in the convent? I've heard they have decadent parties and that men visit, and mad nuns stick their bottoms out of the windows at passers-by.'

Her laughter scatters across the room, drawing attention, but I don't care and laugh too.

'Not the one I was in,' I smile.

'I see,' says Paulina seriously, but her eyes dance impishly. 'Is it true that they torture you with instruments if you do something sinful? And you have to make necklaces out of children's teeth?'

'No,' I say, laughing as I shake my head. 'Nothing like that. It was mainly very, very boring. Anyway, I want to hear about Venice, and parties, and dresses, and – well, everything.'

She smiles and draws a deep breath. I guess she doesn't know where to start.

People who have been friends as children always find a thousand things to say to each other, no matter how long they have been parted. For the rest of the evening Paulina is there, if not right beside me, then hovering nearby. Now that I've found her, it seems that my new life is going to get easier. One day I'll become as confident and self-possessed as she.

'Come,' Paulina beckons, putting out her hands to me. 'Come and dance.'

But a man in a silver-threaded jacket steps between us and puts his hands around my waist. 'I've been trying to summon the courage to talk to this lovely stranger all night.'

His eyes are kind. My heart flutters as I wonder for a moment if he is Vincenzo.

'I don't imagine you're ever short of courage, Pietro,' teases Paulina.

'Oh, but I am,' he replies. 'Every time I ask a lovely girl to dance.'

No, he's not my intended. But the way he smiles down at me makes my cheeks flush.

'So,' says Pietro, 'I must know, this instant, who in heaven's name is this wonderful woman.'

'I'm Laura della Scala.'

'Well, Laura della Scala, I'm Pietro Castellano, and I've discovered my purpose in coming tonight. It's to dance with you.'

He leads me out on to the floor.

I stumble after him, trying to keep up. 'I've never danced,' I tell him.

'Never danced? Where have you been all these years? In a convent?'

'Actually – yes.'

Pietro laughs – I don't think he believes me. 'Anyone can dance. Even a clumsy, awkward fellow like me. Let me show you how.'

He's right. He spends a few minutes slowly taking me through steps that seemed so intricate when I was watching, helping me to learn the simple rhythm that lies underneath. Pietro grips my waist and my left hand, and as we speed around the floor I see our laughing faces reflected in one of the gold-encrusted mirrors. I, Laura della Scala, am dancing – with a man I've only just met!

A firm grip clutches my arm and we halt. It's my father.

'Excuse me, Pietro. I need my daughter.'

'Yes, of course,' Pietro says graciously. He bows to me. 'A pleasure, Laura, an absolute pleasure.'

My father smiles tightly and steers me across the room.

'It strikes me that you need a chaperone,' he says. 'To teach you the way things are done.'

'Father, do you remember Paulina? I've just met her –'

'Yes, yes.' He isn't looking at me any more, but waves to someone in the crowd. 'There's so much you still need to learn.'

'Paulina can teach me,' I say.

My father smiles indulgently. 'Paulina in many ways is more immature than you. It comes from having no father in her life.'

The person he was waving to comes through the throng towards us. It's a young woman. Her face is very pale. She has red-gold hair and aquamarine eyes fringed with dark lashes. Her looks are striking. I recognize her as one of my sister's old friends.

'Is that –'

'Carina!' finishes my father, opening his arms wide.

Carina kisses him on both cheeks, then turns her lovely gaze to me. She gives a sharp cry, raising a hand to her red lips, then sighs.

'I'm sorry,' she says, fanning her face with delicate fingers. 'For a moment I thought . . . You remind me of her so much, Laura.'

Her words make tears start to my eyes. I take her hands and kiss her. 'Thank you,' I say.

'Well, I shall leave you two to reacquaint yourselves,' says my father. 'Laura, be advised in all matters by Carina. She's the perfect guide for a young lady of Venice.'

If Paulina had been my best friend, Carina had been my sister's, one of the many radiant girls who always seemed so aloof when I was little. When she reminds me of her name from those days – de Ferrara – I realize her parents are Julius and Grazia, the black-clad couple thrown out of the party.

'Oh, don't worry!' she says. 'When I married I escaped the talk of vendettas and that nonsense.' She smoothes the white silk of her gown. 'And I cast off my mourning garb long ago.'

She tells that last month she married Count Raffaello – she's a contessa now. She points Raffaello out through the crowd. A fine figure, not tall but with shapely legs and a fierce shock of black hair over a soldier's face – chiselled and broad. He raises a glass at us. Carina blows him a kiss.

I understand why my father wants me to learn from her. Carina's what he aspires for *me* to become. Perhaps there was a measure of kindness in my father's choice too; he must have known that sharing my grief for Beatrice would make it less burdensome. I imagine Carina and Raffaello calling on Vincenzo and me, sitting with us in our courtyard, laughing and sipping wine.

She hooks her alabaster arm through mine. 'Let's sit and talk,' she says. 'How proud your father must be that you're ready to take Beatrice's place.'

I shake my head. 'No one could possibly do that. But I want to honour her memory in whatever way I can.'

'She adored you, Laura. I'm sure you know how much.'

We join Paulina and Pietro, who are resting between dances with a crowd of other young men and girls. Their faces glow.

Carina points to Pietro. 'Young man,' she says playfully,

'take your pack away for a moment. Let the ladies catch their breaths.'

'My pack?' he says, eyes widening in mock innocence. 'You malign us!'

'Hmm,' says Carina. She claps her hands. 'Privacy, please, gentlemen.'

The young men scatter. Carina perches on a cushioned bench, pulling me down beside her. Paulina sits on my other side and the girls gather around us.

'So now,' Carina says, 'lessons for a girl new to society. Let me think – where do I begin? Ah, first we must start with the essential accessory of the Venetian lady.'

She draws a fan from her dress like a weapon: it depicts swallows fluttering in the branches of a cypress tree. Her eyes sparkle.

'Wonderful for staying cool on heated evenings.' says Carina. 'Perfect for secret conversations – especially those about love.'

She holds it in front of her face to reveal only her eyes, batting her lashes coquettishly. Paulina and the other girls giggle.

'The fan,' Carina continues. 'A simple thing, inexpensive and easy to find, but worth a fortune. Make sure you have one for every outfit. But never black and gold. Remember that.'

'Why not black and gold?' I ask her, feeling there are at least a million things I have to learn.

'Because,' Paulina says, 'black and gold is the colour of the Duchess's fan. No matter what she wears, her fan is always black and gold.'

Carina nods. 'The Doge and his wife make all the rules of Venice – as my poor parents will tell you at every opportunity.'

The musicians begin another song and the girls rush to join Pietro and his friends. They seize each other's hands and whirl away in an elaborate dance. Carina, Paulina and I remain seated. They open their spectacular fans wide.

Behind the screen of bone and silk, I learn about the people who pass in front of us. One woman is well known for having affairs with men below her station. Carina says that everyone calls her palazzo 'the boat house', as she entertains so many gondoliers there while her husband is away. There is a man on the verge of financial ruin, desperately trying to call in favours tonight before his entire fortune sinks. His face wears a hunted look. It feels cruel to be speaking of people like this, but I find myself swept along on a tide of gossip and scandal.

I start as Carina and Paulina suddenly snap their fans shut. They stand up, their shoulders draw back. Their features freeze.

An old man walks towards us – older than my father, stooped and thin. I too stand, more slowly. The man grins. Wisps of hair hang like white threads around his ears. Brown age spots are sprinkled over his hands and his face, like blotches of wet rust. Apart from his narrow eyes, which blink and water, the rest of his body seems locked in some sort of paralysis. When he finally speaks, bubbles of spit gather at the corners of his mouth.

'Good evening, Laura,' he says. 'It is I, Vincenzo.'

10

My stomach constricts and I think I might be sick. Father is watching the scene from across the ballroom, and I sense others are too. I grip the red folds of my dress to stop the trembling in my hands. But I have four years of duty to draw upon, and the lessons of the convent serve me well. I curl my lips into a smile and wear my face like a mask.

'Signor,' I say.

Vincenzo grins at me. His mouth is a dark hole. I can see his broken teeth crowded unevenly inside. He bows without taking his eyes away from my face, and then he holds out his arms. 'My dear, won't you join me in this dance?'

Carina and Paulina stare at me.

'Very well,' I reply. I can't see that there's anything else to be done.

We move around the room together. The hands of my last dance partner were gentle and kind, but Vincenzo's feel like monstrous insects crawling around my waist. He's bumping his body up against mine: by accident, perhaps, but maybe not. Three times he steps on my feet and my pale satin slippers become stained by the soles of his black-buckled shoes.

His breath is bitter. I turn my face away.

'Ah,' he rasps, 'you're as shy as your sister was!'

Poor Beatrice. I couldn't blame her for letting me believe she was happy and in love. I imagine what awful things she had kept to herself about this man – this man who holds my future in his disgusting old hands.

Vincenzo tightens his arm around my waist and clutches my hand as though he suspects I might try to escape. Over his bony shoulder I see the partygoers staring at us. Some clap and laugh. Others whisper behind their fans. My father nods approvingly as Vincenzo drags me past him, the crevices of his face seeming deeper and harder.

Vincenzo inches his hand further up my back and I wince.

'Oh, you think I'm too ugly, too old. Is that it, young Laura?'

'No, no,' I say quickly. 'I have a sore foot.'

'Did I stand on your toe, my poor girl? No matter – I shall kiss it better soon.' He stops smiling and sneers, 'Tell me, have you any further complaints about the man who will save your father from penury and shame? The colour of my robes, perhaps, or the speed of my dancing? Come on, little girl, you can tell me.'

I don't say anything. All I can think is that I would gladly become a Bride of Christ right now, and spend the rest of my days polishing altar rails on my knees.

For a moment he stalls in the dance at the edge of the room. 'Good,' he continues. 'My turn, then. First: there are to be no glances, sideways, or any-other-ways for that matter, towards the stupid young boys who'd all like a slice of your soft young skin. Let them long for you.' With a bony finger, he draws an invisible line from my shoulder to the tip of my middle finger. I shudder. 'Second, all you need to worry about is doing what you're told. Obedience is the most attractive feature of the good wife. And I know,' he says, taking my chin in his hand and pinching it until it hurts, 'that you'll make a very good wife.'

I pull away from him. A sour retch rises in my throat. I have to get out. I need some air. As I push through the crowd, running towards the double doors, I hear him call after me. 'Make sure you come back, my dear!'

I run through the marble hallway, past the melancholy statue and startled footmen. I see the masts of boats in the harbour through a door at the end of a long corridor and rush towards them. I step on to a long balcony, pressing my hot hands against the stone balustrades. Deep breaths. I lean over the inky water and let the breeze cool my flushed face.

'Somebody help me,' I whisper. It's an empty prayer because no one can answer it – not Faustina nor Bianca, Paulina or even Carina. I'm alone.

I shiver in the night air, but I'm not ready to go back to the ballroom yet. There's a door at the far end of the balcony, set into the wall of the palace. I walk up to it, turn the heavy metal handle and step through.

Staring down at me, from the top of a wooden scaffold, is the most handsome man I have ever seen.

11

He wears a white paint-splattered shirt that billows at the sleeves. It hangs loose around his neck, revealing the olive skin of his chest. His hair and eyes are almost black, his cheekbones sharp in the lamplight. He looks like an angel.

'I'm sorry,' I stammer, still flustered from the shock of Vincenzo. 'I'll leave.'

'No,' he says quickly, then bows his head. 'I mean, my lady, there's no need.'

On his arm is an oval palette spread with magical colours, and in his hand a long black paintbrush. The scaffold he stands on is next to a wall decorated with a half-finished fresco. It shows the three Magi visiting the Holy Family; the Christ child's halo is picked out in gold leaf and in the background I recognize the domes and towers of Venice. The room is spacious and grand, but the furniture is covered with sheets and the other walls are stripped to bare plaster. A fire burns fiercely in a marble grate. It lights the man's face as he climbs down the scaffolding towards me.

'You're an artist,' I say, and immediately feel foolish.

But he nods and smiles. 'An artist in training. I started by painting portraits for the Doge and his family, and now he's given me other commissions. Like this room.'

His voice is low and gentle. Vincenzo, my father and the ball all seem very far away.

'It must be wonderful to have a talent like that,' I say. 'Have you studied for a long time?'

'Less than some,' he says. 'I used to want to be a mathematician. Although art and logic are just different ways of doing the same things.'

'What kinds of things?'

'Oh, you know, uncovering beautiful patterns, making sense of the world, shining light on important moments.'

He stands at a wooden trestle table crowded with pots of paint, powdered pigment and brushes. Carefully, he adds a pinch of yellow pigment to blue and brown, making a smooth olive green. It's so peaceful in here; I don't want to go back just yet.

'Do you mind if I watch you work?' I ask.

'I'd like that,' he says.

He pulls one of the sheets away to reveal a wooden chair, its seat upholstered with leather and its feet moulded into lion's claws. I sink into it and he daubs the olive paint on to his palette.

'Too much dancing?' he asks.

'I'm not very good,' I answer.

He nods sympathetically, and continues to apply his paint to the palette. The silence swells, and I can't help but tap my toes together like a little girl.

'Have you always lived in Venice?' I ask him.

'Well, I lived in the city as a child, but I've been away for some years. I've only recently returned.'

'Me too,' I tell him. 'I'm learning my way around again. It's all a mystery to me at the moment.'

He climbs up the scaffolding and sits on the platform at the top. Dipping his brush into the paint, he outlines the foliage at the edge of the fresco with delicate strokes.

'Venice is a city of secrets,' he says. 'Everyone seems to have one.'

I think of my father's dwindling estate; Beatrice's pretence about Vincenzo; the Doge's sickness.

He leans back to look at the finished leaf. 'But what would I know of secrets? I'm just a painter.'

'You don't have any?' I ask.

His gentle eyes settle on mine. He pauses for a moment, but then grins and points to the centre of the fresco, where the Virgin Mary stands. The Christ Child is in her arms, her eyes are turned up to heaven. She wears an intensely blue robe – bluer than the midday sky or the brightest of sapphires. 'I'm the only painter in Venice who knows how to make that colour. It's why the Doge likes my work.'

'How do you make it?' I ask.

He rests his chin in his hand, his dancing eyes narrowed as he pretends to consider my question.

'I won't tell anyone,' I insist. 'I swear.'

'Well, then . . .' He gestures to me to come closer. I stand on the bottom rung of the scaffolding and he whispers down to me. 'First you must strain water through the finest muslin, until it's perfectly pure. Gently crush lapis lazuli, and mix it with walnut oil. Pour the water over them, and leave the mixture to mingle overnight.'

I shake my head. 'No wonder none of the other painters have discovered it.'

He looks at me for a little while. 'Oh no!' he says, almost under his breath, though a smile plays at the corners of his red lips.

'What?' I ask.

'I've put myself in your power now. Can I trust you?' His eyes hold me.

'Of course –'

The door swings open and we both turn at the same time. It's Carina.

'Laura! I've been searching all over the palazzo for you. The footmen saw you come this way . . .' She glances up at the painter, who stands quickly, moving away from me. 'I was starting to worry. Come back to the ball. There are still so many people I want you to meet!'

She takes me by the hand, pulls me through the door. When I look back at him, he's watching me, his hands on his hips.

Carina hurries me along the corridor. She murmurs, 'One moment you're in a convent, the next you're consorting with servants in back rooms! Goodness, what would your father say?'

I know she's only teasing me, but I think I hear a hiss of disapproval in her words.

12

I was sure it would rain on the morning of my sister's funeral. I was sure that the birds would fall silent and that the flowers would turn their gaudy faces away.

But everything is resplendent – the sky is the same blue I saw in the half-painted fresco. Turtledoves sing in the trees. Huge peonies show themselves off like the wanton women who stalk the lanes behind St Mark's Square.

As often as I try to close my thoughts off to Vincenzo, he sneaks back in. I feel guilty for dwelling on my own predicament on such a sorrowful day as today. Though I hate to think it, there's even a tiny part of me that feels anger towards my dead sister for leaving me to this fate. Not that I could wish it on any other.

I escape to the courtyard. Faustina and Bianca have put me in a long, wide-skirted black-taffeta dress. It rustles and swishes like trees in a storm. I want to be calm and quiet on my own, but the ripple of voices reaches me from the other side of the wall Beatrice and I used to play on. One of them is Bianca's, and the other sounds like a little girl. They laugh quietly. I move towards them, leaves and twigs catching on my dress.

'Look,' says Bianca. 'A few stitches here and there and it really will look like no one's worn it. I'll be able to walk down to the Lido and people will think I'm a real Venetian lady!'

I step up on the bench and peer over the wall. Bianca is holding a gown of yellow silk that pours over her knees like melted gold – the dress Beatrice drowned in. A sob escapes from me. Bianca looks up as a small child jumps from her side.

'Signorina della Scala. Good afternoon – I mean, I'm sorry.' The little girl scampers off and Bianca squashes the dress into her sewing basket. 'I didn't mean you to see . . . Your father said I could have it. Shouldn't you be at the graveside?'

I look away from the gaudy silk. 'The funeral hasn't started yet,' I say and I turn away.

As I move back to the house, I hear Faustina's shouts.

'Laura! Laura! Laura!' She comes puffing into the courtyard, hitching up her black apron. She holds my face with her big, worn hands. They are warm and comforting, and part of me feels like the very small girl I once was. 'We must join your father.'

The coffin is carried from the chapel of Saint Helena by six stone-faced men in dark cloaks. I'm at my father's side, Faustina behind. Lysander has been told the news by letter, but it may not even have reached him yet. The black snake of mourners processes towards its destination – the burial ground. When we reach it a great mob of sympathizers has already arrived, waiting to shake my father's hand. He presses his lips together and nods his head, thanking everyone for coming. Every so often he turns to me with a mournful smile, but I can't find any comfort in it.

The mourners' empty mantras and useless truths of condolence wash over me. A man introduces himself as Carlito, my father's cousin. He tells me how sorry he is, and that his wife wishes she was well enough to join us. I murmur my thanks. A toothless old woman whom I don't recognize wheezes, 'She was an angel. Such a terrible loss,' and then shuffles off, coughing loudly.

I know they are being kind, these people who come to mourn with us, but most of them remind me of cockroaches, clustering together in little groups, scuttling up the avenue to pay their clacking respects.

'I wish they'd all go away,' I whisper to Faustina.

'We must grieve in public, my dear. It's what we must do,' she replies, pressing a handkerchief into my hand.

I stand at the head of Beatrice's grave. The grass and flowers have been wrenched away from the hole where her body will go. Broken stalks poke out of the torn ground in tufts. The priest's robe flutters as chants: 'May perpetual light ever shine upon her. May she rest in peace. May the saints soothe her, may Jesus's tears heal her, may the Mother of God cradle her in her loving arms.'

I feel a dark shadow at my shoulder. Vincenzo is there, like a vulture, stooping and rubbing his hands together. He leans close to me and I feel his hot breath on my neck.

'Here, at the edge of death,' he says, 'we sow the seeds of future happiness for us and for your family. Isn't that a wonderful thing for us to do, Laura?'

They put the lid on her coffin. They lower Beatrice deep down into the cold ground, where no light will ever penetrate and no birds will ever sing. Beside us, three solemn-faced women play harps decorated with gilt cherubs. The notes soar above us, but instead of the sounds of angels I simply hear the snap and twang of the strings.

I stand by Beatrice's grave while my father wishes farewell to the other attendees. My eyes are filmed with tears; when I pass my handkerchief over them I see that I am not completely alone. A woman with silver-grey hair and a regal bearing approaches. Allegreza di Rocco – the woman I met at the Doge's palazzo.

'Laura,' she says gently. 'May I talk with you for a moment, child?'

I nod.

Allegreza takes my arm and we move along the path, away from my father and the others. The gnarled cypress trees bend above us and the gravestones lean and lurk.

'Your father thinks it's your duty to marry that horrible old man,' she says.

The anger in her voice startles me and I pull my arm away from hers.

Allegreza strokes my cheek. 'Don't be afraid,' she tells me. 'This match between you and Vincenzo goes against the laws of nature. There's not a woman in Venice who doesn't feel for you. I can help, if you listen very carefully. Tonight, as soon after midnight as you can, you must come to see us.'

She takes my hand and presses a slip of parchment into my palm.

'Once you have read this, burn it. Do you understand?'
'Yes,' I say, even though I understand nothing at all.
'And tell no one,' she adds.

13

'My appointment to the Grand Council is practically guaranteed now!'

My father smiles. His teeth and lips are stained dark from many glasses of wine, making him look fierce and slightly frenzied. 'Laura, can you imagine what this means?'

I can't, but I say, 'Yes, Father,' and push the grilled sardines across my plate.

'Lysander's no good,' he says, jabbing the air with his fork. 'Nose stuck in books and potions. But you're a good girl. And your sister was a good girl, and I am a fortunate man.' His gestures have become large and sloppy. He knocks his glass against my plate, and murmurs an apology to his wine.

I feel inside the pocket of my dress for the scrap of parchment Allegreza handed to me. *The monastery at San Michele*, it reads. Beneath the lettering is the symbol of a key. I see Allegreza's strong noble face inside my head and wonder whether it is wisdom or folly to do as she asks.

'There's so much we must prepare for the wedding.' He's slurring his words. 'And then you'll be busy afterwards, with the demands of the bridal bower!'

As I understand what he means, my appetite leaves me. The doubts I had about Allegreza evaporate completely.

As St Mark's bell tower strikes a distant eleven o'clock, I watch the parchment catch alight in the candle flame. I throw it into the hearth.

I dress quickly and silently. Bianca has finished converting one of Beatrice's warm gowns into a new cape, and she's draped it over the chair beside my bed. Midnight blue lined with bright purple satin, it slides soothingly against my arms. I tiptoe to my door and wince when it creaks open. I flip the silky hood over my head and I pray to the Blessed Virgin Mary – even though I'm almost positive she won't approve of what I'm doing. I creep past my father's door, down the marble staircase and into his library. I scoop up a few coins from a platter on his desk and pour the tinkling handful into my velvet purse. I bite my lip as I open the side door of the palazzo and slip through.

In the dark, I run down towards the canal, scuffing the ground with my shoes. Shadows cast spindly shapes on the pavements and the walls as I hurry past, my hooded head down. The licking and lapping of the black water sounds like a slurping, hungry beast. A strain of distant singing floats through the air. *Calma. Calma.*

A gondolier leans against the dock, idly stirring the water.

'Signor?'

Though fear courses through my blood, it occurs to me that I've never before given instructions to a man.

'Can you take me to St Michele? The monastery?'

He frowns. 'On the north shore, isn't it?'

I nod, although I have no idea. I hope he's right.

'I'm in a hurry,' I say.

He stares at me curiously, then offers me his arm. I lean on it and climb aboard.

'Only so fast a gondola can go,' he says, 'but I'll make it as quick as I can.'

He sets off, pushing his oar against the side of the canal with a low *clunk*. In the glossy dark, with the night lights of Venice winking at me, I feel a shiver of freedom tingle down my spine. This is the first time in my life that I have chosen my own path.

I almost enjoy the journey. To the south, the domes and the turrets rise up from our waterborne city, silvery white against the dark sky. The gondolier swirls the dark waters beneath us, driving the boat forward in a way that feels half magical. We turn the corner of one of the northern canals and cross the lagoon.

'What's a young girl like you doing, anyway, rushing across the water at night?' he asks. His voice is not unkind, though, and I try to sound like I'm on normal business.

'I have an aunt. She's old and sick. She's been asking for me.'

'Well, you're a good niece to be going to her at this hour of the night. I hope it's nothing serious.'

'So do I,' I reply.

Ahead of us hulks an island. The boat rocks in the choppy current as slowly, slowly, it looms closer. From its centre the dome of the monastery and its bell tower rise into a purple-black sky.

He steers us closer. The building's long low wall isn't flanked by any pathways and the water laps at its base. At first I can't see a way in, but as we draw nearer I realize that there are low gates embedded far down the wall. Small torches, which don't shed much light, glimmer tentatively on either side. My gondolier slips his craft through the watery gateway, and we are inside.

The landing place is beside a castellated courtyard. Pillars and arches form a sheltered walkway. It's utterly silent, save for the perpetual slap of water against stone.

The gondolier stares around us. 'Would you like me to come with you?'

'No, no, thank you, sir. But I would be grateful if you could wait. I'll try not to be too long.'

He looks uncertain, so I hand him a coin. 'Please.'

He lays down his oar. 'Take as much time as you need. I'm sure your aunt will be the better for your visit.'

He helps me out of the boat and I step up on to a great plateau of black and white marble. It stretches from the canal to the walls of the monastery like a giant chessboard. The water reflects on its surface and the marble wobbles and shimmers.

I walk towards the covered walkway. All is silent, dark and still. An unnatural breeze whips my cape, something flaps past, and I crouch to the ground with my hood pulled around my head. Just a bird – a disturbed gull, perhaps – but it makes me pant like an animal.

'Pull yourself together,' I whisper to myself. That's what the Abbess would have said if she had seen me cowering and shaking like this.

A giant doorway made of cracked wood is set into the

monastery's walls. It's studded with dull metal bolts, each as round and large as a man's fist. Seaweed creeps up the hem of the building, green and slippery fronds feeling their way out of the deep.

The door opens. Too late to leave. A man in a brown hooded robe emerges, his face obscured. He beckons silently with a curled finger.

'I'm Laura,' I say to him and he nods his head as if this is something he already knows.

I follow him down a narrow corridor lined with sconces spaced far apart. Between them, in the darkest places, I can hardly see my feet. The shadow of my companion's cowl stretches and retracts as we come in proximity to the torches. We turn several corners. A right, another right, then a left. We climb a stone spiral staircase. I worry that I won't be able to find my way back.

'Excuse me,' I ask. 'Where are we going?'

He doesn't reply.

At the top of the stairs we emerge into a cavernous hall. Heat and light almost stings my face. I'm blinded and dazzled. As my eyes adjust, I see gold on the walls and frescoes of deep blue and ferocious red. The man has already slipped away.

A cluster of figures, perhaps fifteen women, stand beside one of the four fires that blaze in hearths taller than them. Each wears a long robe and has a mask on her face, but I can somehow sense they are all women. I feel my skin tightening and despite the warmth of the room, I shiver. What is this place?

The figures glide forward and form a circle around me. Their masks cast flickering, grotesque shadows. Some have long, hooked beaks, like birds of prey. Gauze butterfly wings drift softly from others. Their jewels and lace and feathers frame eyes that pierce me like a hunter's arrows. The air is filled with a dizzying scent of spice and wood smoke. But there's something else too – something more powerful and pungent than any of that.

My heart gallops. *This is a trap*, I think.

One of the figures reaches towards me and I shrink away, my eyes flicking round for a way out. The woman laughs from behind her feathery mask. The whole group moves closer, tightening the ring.

'What do you want from me?' I say. 'Who are you?'

A tall woman steps forward. The hair within her hood is streaked with grey. Her mask is shaped like the face of a white owl, covered in white jewels and with a silver beak. She removes it, and Allegreza's eyes glitter in the firelight.

'Welcome, Laura,' she says, 'to the Segreta.'

14

The Segreta. The Secret Ones. The hiss and bite of the word sends a chill across my skin.

'You said you could help me,' I say, squeezing my fists and digging my nails into my palms to stop me from shaking.

'We can,' says Allegreza. 'But there are rules.' The women nod. 'And there is a price.'

There's always a price, I think, remembering my father's words that day he left me at the convent.

'Have you told anyone of your visit here?' Allegreza asks.

I shake my head.

'That is the first rule.' Her voice is a stony whisper. 'Our organization must remain in the shadows.' There's a murmur of approval. 'The second rule is just as important. If you want us to help you, you must give us something.'

I rummage in the folds of my dress and pull out my velvet purse. 'I'm not sure if this is enough.'

Allegreza smiles and waves it aside with a long, pale hand. 'We would be a mundane society indeed if all we wanted was your money.' The women's masks shake as their wearers titter.

'No – we're looking for something more precious and more powerful than coins or jewels.'

'What do you mean?' I ask.

'Why,' she says, drawing out the word, 'we want a secret.'

The women step even closer towards me, like a hungry pack. There is no way through the press of their robed bodies. Their eyes glint from behind their masks and I wonder what they will do if I can't give them what they want.

A secret? For years I've done nothing but stitch, and pray, and sing. I scour my brain for something that no one else knows. My father and his financial worries? That's no good. One glance at our faded palazzo tells the tale. The Abbess's fondness for wine? I can't be sure that rumour isn't simply Annalena's mischief. The herbal remedies prepared by the convent, which cure people of all manner of dreadful things? But women all over Italy have their own potions. I've no secrets to reveal, no proper ones. Nothing that will persuade the Segreta to save me from Vincenzo.

I can't look at them now. I lower my eyes to the stone at my feet. 'I don't have any secrets.'

Sudden laughter fills the room, echoing among the stone archways. I stare at the women, bewildered. What have I said that's so funny?

I feel my cheeks flush. I'm not frightened any more, but cross that I'm being mocked. It's been a ridiculous journey. I ought to leave, though I'm not sure I can find my way back to the gondola on my own.

The last of the laughter dies away and Allegreza cocks her head.

'Everyone has a secret,' she says. 'We can't help you if you don't tell us yours.'

'Come on, Laura,' says a golden-haired woman in a fox's mask. 'There are plenty of girls we could help instead. Don't waste our time.'

I'm a beggar with nothing to offer. Surely Allegreza could have seen that when she first met me. Just a girl, empty of secrets. And now empty of hope. The bitter air of Vincenzo's breath forms a cloud above me. For I'm sure now that I will have to marry him.

'I should leave,' I say.

Allegreza's mouth is a stern, straight line and the great room is filled with a throbbing kind of silence until she speaks again. 'Very well.'

The circle of women opens and I slip out. I can sense their eyes on my back as I walk towards the spiral staircase. I've failed. My mind is already travelling forward in time, anticipating the difficult task of getting to bed again without being seen. I walk down the steps, steadying myself against the cold wall with one hand. There's a doorway, and I go through it, finding myself in an unlit chamber. This isn't the way I came. I go back to the staircase and continue my way down. But the next chamber doesn't look any more familiar than the last. Wretched place. Will I now face the ignominy of having to return to the Segreta and ask directions?

I lean my shoulder against the stairwell. Tears of frustration wet my eyes and I curl my hand into a fist, striking the wall. The floor rings with a jangling sound and I realize that my sudden movement has sent my purse tumbling from my dress.

The coins spin and rattle down the steps. Mary, mother of God! I tell myself to take deep breaths.

I half crawl, half stoop to gather up as many as I can find. My purse lies in a pool of starlight, and I funnel the coins back into it. The last one in my palm is larger than the rest – a gold ducat. Engraved on it is St Mark, a flapping banner in his hands, which he hands to the figure opposite – the Doge.

In that moment, I remember that I do have a secret. A secret worth far more than the coins in my purse, or even Vincenzo's fortune.

'*I'm a weak man. Weak and yielding. No one in Venice can find out what I suffer.*'

A whispering voice of uncertainty tells me I should keep the promise I made to him. But my heart's roar drowns it out. I have no choice.

I hitch up my skirts and run back up the twisting stairs. I see the glow cast from the enormous fireplaces and rush into the room. I feel armed – like I'm carrying a sword.

The women stand or sit in small groups, but they turn as one at the sound of my footsteps.

'What are you doing?' snaps the woman in the fox mask. 'You have made your –'

'I have one!' I interrupt. 'I have a secret.'

15

'Don't test us further, child,' says Allegreza.

'I'm not,' I insist, shaking my head. My breath is ragged from running here, but I'm certain of what I'm about to say. 'My secret concerns the Doge.'

Allegreza stiffens. 'You know that his wife, the Duchess, is my cousin? Tread carefully. This is not a place for scurrilous gossip.'

I tell them my secret. Of the falling sickness, of his thrashing as the demons take over. My words tumble over each other, and I spare no detail of his affliction, or my own part in the story.

The Segreta inhale one huge collective gasp. Someone claps her hands. Murmurs, whispers and little yelps scatter through the air.

Allegreza holds up her hand. 'Silence!'

There is a hush again.

'My dear,' she says. There's a softness in her face even though the fiery glow still flickers fiercely all around us, dancing in her eyes. She moves closer. 'This is true?'

'Yes, yes. I promise.' I add, 'He doesn't want anyone to know.'

The room is silent for a moment. 'Then why have you told us?' asks Allegreza, smiling.

Is this some sort of trick? A test? She knows why.

'I thought you could help me,' I say.

'So you prize your own wellbeing above the oath you made to the Doge?'

'I . . .'

'Go on.'

I'm not sure if I'm being teased or reprimanded. I glance round at the other women, but any clue they might give is hidden behind their masks.

I whisper, 'Yes.' What else can I do?

Allegreza stares into my eyes. I set my jaw, determined not to lower my eyes. Finally, she nods. 'Very well, then. We must assess the value of your contribution. Wait here.'

She leads the women off between a pair of arches, into a side chamber. They process like nuns on their way to holy prayers. I glimpse a big wooden table and three lighted candelabras. Then they close the door and I am alone.

What have I done? Marrying Vincenzo remains a disgusting prospect, but by being here, I feel that I might be getting tangled in an even more terrible web.

I wonder what the hour is. I walk over to one of the thin windows to see if the air is lightening, or if there are dawn streaks of pink and orange in the sky. Beatrice once wrote that sometimes our father prowls through the palazzo at night, pacing up and down and muttering to himself. I wonder if he's creeping about on the other side of the lagoon, looking into my room and discovering I am gone.

The door opens and the women pour back into the room. Allegreza stands before me, her white owl mask back in place.

'Laura, men have always governed women – whether at home, when a husband gives orders to his wife, or in the complex machinations of the Grand Council. Men say they rule by the grace of God, but the source of their power is hypocrisy, vice and corruption. The Segreta is a tonic to this poison. By meeting here, we determine the fortunes of Venice. Men may be princes, priests, even the Doge, but the strings that control them are in our hands.'

A rush of excitement flows through me. I think I may have turned the key to the door of my freedom.

'If his enemies knew the secret you have given us,' continues Allegreza, 'the Doge would be in great danger. News of his sickness would spread like a plague of its own. His opponents would use it to challenge him; to topple him from power.' Her voice lowers. 'Do you see, Laura? A secret can cut deeper than any blade.'

'But I don't want anyone to hurt the Doge,' I say. 'He seems a kind man.'

A woman with a mask like a scaly python laughs. 'Men seem many things.'

'In return for what you have given us,' Allegreza interrupts, 'we will stop your marriage to Vincenzo.'

I clasp my hands to my breast. Relief bubbles inside me. 'Thank you,' I breathe.

Allegreza holds her hand out to me and I take it. She slides her other hand beneath the folds of her robe and draws out something long and thin. For a moment I think she's holding a folded-up fan. But when the firelight lends it a metallic gleam, I feel a chill on my skin and everything inside me tightens.

A knife.

'No!' I mutter.

I see everything clearly. They have my secret now, and no more use for me. I try to yank my hand free, but Allegreza's grip is strong.

'Don't be afraid,' she says. 'This will only hurt a little.'

She positions the tip of the knife in the centre of my palm. I feel a sharp sting at first, but nothing more. A bead of blood forms and trickles across my skin.

'Welcome to the Segreta,' Allegreza says.

The wound is nothing, an inconsequential stigma, but she reaches once more beneath her robe, and this time takes out a lace-edged handkerchief with which she gently binds my hand. The woman wearing the fox mask steps forward – a shimmering mass of pearls and creamy feathers in her hands. It's a swan mask. Sparkling beads of jet edge its eyes, and an elegant ochre beak follows a smooth line to where it joins the ghostly forehead.

Allegreza takes it. I raise my chin and she slowly lowers it over my face. She puts a hand on my shoulder, turning me round, then knots the satin ribbons together to hold it in place. It has the aromatic smell of another woman's perfume, and I know at once I'm not the first to wear it.

'The meeting is concluded,' says Allegreza.

She walks me back outside, taking a different, shorter route than the way I arrived. A bluish fog rises from the water and I can see the first fingers of dawn touching the domes and towers of the city. She carefully arranges my cape around me, but her eyes flash fiercely behind her mask.

'We will keep our promise,' she says, 'but remember yours. You're one of us, now. Breathe one word of the Segreta to anyone – and your life will be forfeit.'

'I won't tell a soul,' I say.

She squeezes my hand before melting back into the shadows.

I stand alone on the giant chessboard, my hot breath caught inside the mask.

You're one of us. But who were the Segreta? Apart from Allegreza, I had no idea. I felt bile rise inside me as I imagined the plots and crimes they might be hatching right now, in this shrouded monastery. I've been a fool. I've undermined the most powerful man in Venice, and for what? They have taken my secret, weighed its value, and like a crooked merchant, deferred the return payment. I've nothing to show for my visit except an empty promise.

I untangle the ribbons behind my head, pull the mask from my face and cast it on the ground. I gulp at the cold air. The mask stares from the chequered stone, glowing like a spectre. No – I can't leave it for the Segreta to find. I snatch it up, shoving it under my cloak.

At the water's edge, the gondolier is waiting.

'Your aunt not any better?' he asks, studying my face as he helps me into the boat.

I don't answer. I pull my cape around me and we glide back across the shimmering lagoon.

16

It is almost daylight when I reach home. I tiptoe up the stairs, holding my skirts around my thighs to stop them swishing. My father's room is still closed and the palazzo silent. In my room I untie the handkerchief from my hand, and see a small scab has already formed. I quickly pull the mask from my cape and slip it inside one of the chests of drawers. I gather a pile of silk shawls that were Beatrice's and arrange them on top. I rub my eyes, exhausted.

I throw off my cape and shoes and peel my dress over my head, thinking that I'll pull my covers over me and not think about the Segreta until the morning. I'm just about to slip into bed when I see, with a start, that someone is sleeping there already.

It's Faustina. I put my hand on her shoulder and shake her gently. She sits up and looks at me for a moment like I'm a stranger. And then her face crumples in relief.

'Thanks be to God!' she says, hugging me tightly and kissing my forehead. 'Where have you been? Oh, I'm so cross with you.'

'I'm all right,' I tell her.

'Where on earth did you go, darling? I've been sick thinking about what might have happened to you. I almost woke your father.'

'I'm glad you didn't do that,' I say. 'Please don't tell him.'

She looks at me with tired eyes. 'You must get into bed. How late it is. Laura, you can't simply disappear from the house. I was beside myself. Oh, the terrible prayers I've been offering to get you home safely.'

'Your prayers have been answered,' I say, giving her a squeeze. 'I'm perfectly fine.'

Faustina smoothes the crumpled sheets and I clamber in. When I was very young, she would pretend to daub my eyelids with enchanted honey, just before I went to sleep. My eyes feel heavy, like they used to then. I want to sleep and find out that the monastery, Allegreza and the Segreta were all a dream, and that no mask lurks in the drawer.

But a sudden quiver from Faustina makes me sit bolt upright. She covers her face with her knobbled hands and a sob rises up from somewhere deep within her. I reach up, pulling her to sit down beside me, and wrap my arms around her plump shoulders.

'I'm sorry,' she gasps between sobs. 'Not being able to find you made me think of your poor dear sister.'

'I'm the one who needs to say sorry. I didn't mean to frighten you.'

She shakes her head. 'It's my fault,' she says. 'All my fault. Beatrice would be here now if only I had stayed with her.'

'It's not your fault,' I say, kissing her wet cheek. 'You mustn't blame yourself.'

'You don't understand,' she says. 'You can't.' She slips from the bed on to her knees and clasps her hands in front of her, her eyes turned up towards heaven. 'God spare me!'

Her invocation seems to tear through her. I've not seen Faustina like this before. There's a wild darkness in her, and it frightens me.

'Faustina, please . . . Beatrice drowned. God won't pass judgement on you for her death. It was an accident!'

'No,' she mumbles. 'It was not.'

A cold breeze seems to snake into the room and coil around me. I sit hunched in the bed, trembling.

'What did you say?'

Faustina turns towards me. Her kind old face is twisted and anguished, as if she too has been wearing a mask.

'Beatrice went somewhere that night,' she says. 'And I was the one who let her go.'

'Go where?' I think the blood inside me has stopped flowing.

'I don't know. You see, she begged me. She kept saying, "There's something I need to do. Please, you must trust me . . ." And I . . . There was hope in her face – hope I hadn't seen since her engagement. So I let her go. God forgive me, I let her go.'

Her voice cracks and she rocks back and forth. I push away the sheets and sit on the floor beside her. I take her hand.

'Faustina . . . do you think she had a secret lover?'

'What else could it have been?'

What else, indeed? A smile pulls at the corners of my mouth. Despite everything, I am glad that old Vincenzo was not the only man Beatrice had known. I imagine her, eyes gleaming, darting into the shadows to share a furtive embrace and words of longing with some beautiful boy who made her heart flutter, who warmed her flesh with kisses.

'I waited for her at the Rialto Bridge, just as I had promised,' says Faustina. 'She said she wouldn't be late and I was starting to worry. That's when I heard her awful scream and that dreadful splash.' She twists the sheet that hangs over my bed and I brush hair away from her face. 'It was a little further up the bank. I ran as though my legs were young again, cursing my old knees and hips. When I got to her, she was still struggling. I see the bubbles and the foam around her in my sleep. Her dress, which I had put on her earlier, had become huge and full in the water. I flung down my shawl. I was at the canal edge, about to jump in to gather her back to me, and then . . . then . . .'

Faustina shuts her crinkly eyes. I put my hand on her shoulder.

'What happened?' I ask gently.

Her eyes open again with an anxious focus. 'Somebody stopped me. A hand clutched my neck. Another seized my wrist and jerked my arm behind my back. It was a man, dragging me away from the canal. I screamed and kicked, but he pressed a knife to my throat.'

'Who was it?' My voice is hoarse.

'I don't know,' she says, trembling. 'Oh, I was so afraid. He leaned close to my ear and whispered, "Let her go, old woman, or you'll join her." And then I could see, under the shadow of his wide black hat, his mouth was full of gold. Little golden knives instead of teeth.'

She breaks into more sobbing and I pull her head against me chest. The image she has conjured is more like a monster than a man.

'He pushed me to the ground, and I shut my eyes. I was a coward, shivering there like a baby. When I realized he had gone, it was too late. A gondolier heard my screams and fished Beatrice from the water.'

My sister was murdered.

This man with golden teeth took Beatrice from me. It's too much to take in. I find my own eyes are dry of tears, though they burn with anger. Who could do such a thing? And why?

17

The morning of my wedding day is just as it should be: cold and stark. My heart is as dead as a cold gravestone. This is the last time I shall sleep alone; tonight, Vincenzo's withered body, shuddering with lust, will be beside me. I was a *fool*. How could I be so naive as to think those women could help me? Would I visit one of the jewellery shacks in the artisan quarter and hand over my money on the promise of delivery the next day? Of course not! Yet that is exactly what I've done. I've betrayed the trust of a good man for nothing.

'You can't lie there all day,' Faustina says, shouldering her way into the room for the third or fourth time that morning. She's gathering the remnants of my mother's life, long gone, assembling my trousseau. The large box of dark wood and gold that sits open in the corner, like the mouth of a monster, is filling up. She feeds it with folded sheets, ornate dresses, fragile twinkling veils, heavy linens. All I will need for my bridal bed. Faustina's movements are heavy and reluctant, as if she's preparing me not for a marriage, but for an execution.

The old woman leaves once more. She seems to have recovered from the tumult of the night before, and her lack of curiosity riles me. If what she says is true – and I've no reason to doubt her – a murderer walks the streets having taken my dear sister's life. I want to question every man, woman and child in Venice until I have him snared.

I sit up as I hear my father's leaden footsteps outside and the door crashes open.

'Jesus Christ Almighty,' he bellows. His hair's unkempt and his doublet unfastened.

'What is it?' I ask.

He stomps straight past me and opens my trousseau chest, packed so carefully by Faustina. He grabs the linen and garments inside, flinging everything out, their neat folds collapsing like blossom ripped from the trees.

'Father!' I gasp. 'What are you doing?'

Bianca lurks outside the door. To my amazement, the young maidservant seems to be suppressing a fit of giggles. Faustina clamps Bianca to her chest, muffling her, and mouths something at me.

My father lifts up the empty chest and hurls it to the floor. The wood cracks and splinters and Bianca lets out a snort from among the folds of Faustina's dress.

'That traitor!' he roars. 'He's a spy! A damned *spy*!'

A tiny spark of hope ignites in my heart. 'Who do you mean, Father?'

'Sneaking off to the Duke of Milan himself!' He paces past me to the other side of the room, and pounds a fist against the wall. 'After all I have done to save the della Scala name.'

'Vincenzo?' I ask.

For the first time, his eyes light on me, and he sinks on to the bed. 'Gone are my chances with the Grand Council,' he says, slapping his knee. 'Gone!'

I pull a solemn, serious look over my face like a veil. 'Vincenzo is a spy?'

'May he rot in Hell!' my father spits. He glances up to where Faustina and Bianca stand staring by the door. 'Get out, both of you!'

Faustina's eyes twinkle as she pulls Bianca away.

My father signs and buries his face in his hands, and the spark in my chest bursts into a flame.

He tells me that letters have been unearthed, witnesses called. They attest that Vincenzo has been acting as an agent for the Duke of Milan for at least two years, feeding information from the meetings of the Grand Council. The evidence is, apparently, incontrovertible. Vincenzo attempted to flee the city with his money chests early this morning, but was captured. His wealth, what the authorities can lay their hands on, will be confiscated; exile is a certainty.

Only halfway through my father's tortured explanation do I see clearly who is responsible for my good fortune. My fingertips move over the rough scab on the inside of my hand. For it can't be fortune at all, but the work of the Segreta. Allegreza has kept her promise.

'I must meet with the Council,' my father mutters, smoothing down his hair. 'I need to distance myself from this scoundrel Vincenzo.'

He leaves the room, and it strikes me that not once did he commiserate with me on the collapse of my marriage. I grin, feeling light-headed. Perhaps he always knew how much I loathed the prospect.

Once his steps have receded, Faustina and Bianca reappear at the door.

'Oh, my darling, you're saved!' cries Faustina, her face flushed with happiness. I leap from my bed to hug her. Bianca throws her arms around us both.

'Saved for now,' I say. 'Father will no doubt be looking for another suitable match when all this has died down.'

'Yes, but for now you're safe,' says Faustina.

'You told me that marriage was for the best,' I remind her, arching my eyebrow.

My old nurse starts to pick up the broken chest and its contents. She looks up and there's the hint of a smile on her lips. 'Did I say that?' she replies, all innocence. 'Well, forgive me. Anyhow, who knows what eligible bachelors will be vying for your hand?'

I'm sprawled among a pile of cushions in the salon downstairs, leafing through my mother's book of Roman love poems. Faustina sits in a leather chair across the room, dozing, her embroidery half fallen from her hand. A rumble of shouts and cries breaks the afternoon peace, and I realize that crowds are lining the road that runs towards the harbour. I close the book, shake my skirts down and go to push one of the windows open and look outside.

'What is it?' asks Faustina sleepily.

'I'm going to find out.' I rush from the salon, towards the back door.

'Don't, darling, this could be dangerous,' Faustina pleads.

'I won't go further than the rear gates,' I call back.

Faustina follows me. With an exasperated sigh, she wraps her shawl about her shoulders and tells me she's coming too.

We hurry down to the gates, past Beatrice's bench, our stone wall and the whispers of the cypress trees. The noise grows louder. Guards shout and jostle the spectators, swords glinting. People spit and roar.

'Stand back!' bellows one of the guards. 'Make way!'

A carriage clatters down the road. A man bursts from the crowd and smacks his hand on the door, shouting 'Traitor!' Others hurl curses and insults, their faces red with anger and excitement. I hoist myself up on the iron bars of the gate so I can see above the furious blur of people. When the carriage passes, I catch a glimpse of the occupant.

It's Vincenzo. Even my brief flicker of a glance shows him ashen. He stares at me for a moment, eyes brimming with a deathly dismay.

I stand tall as I stare back at him. Power thrills through me as he turns away, eyes downcast in shame. Faustina is standing on the bench, and as we watch the carriage clatter away, I realize the truth of Allegreza's words. In Venice, a secret is indeed more powerful than a sword.

18

For the first time since I returned to my father's house, I sleep properly. Deep and heavy and dreamless. When I open my eyes the sun has inched across my bed. I'm free of Vincenzo. And I know what I must do now. I'll find out what happened to my sister. I'll get to the truth.

The Segreta is as powerful as Allegreza promised. I feel like my veins have swollen inside my body. I think I hear the hot red blood rushing through them. I'm alert and wide-eyed. I can smell the air, picking up clues and hints in it that I have not sensed before.

Faustina flaps into my room.

'Sweetheart, there's no time for snoozing! Count Raffaello will be here soon.' She rummages in my chest of clothes and pulls out a pale orange and cream dress.

Count Raffaello, I remember. *Carina's husband*.

'And Carina too?' I ask, climbing out of bed.

'Yes,' Faustina nods. 'It will be nice to have her in the palazzo again – she was such a good friend to dear Beatrice.'

I splash my face and neck in the bowl of water resting by the window. It is scented with roses, and a few red petals float on the surface. I dry myself with a linen cloth and Faustina helps me into the dress. She ties the silken threads that hang from the sleeves and gathers my hair on to my head, fixing it in place with a pearly clasp.

She brings me to the mirror again, where I'm getting used to seeing someone different. I tuck a stray lock behind my ear.

The front door creaks open in the hall below us, and I hear Bianca's voice. 'Greetings, sir.'

'They're here,' says Faustina.

I hurry out of my room and along the passageway. The shutters of the palazzo are wide open and the rooms thrum with light. The dusty air that used to muffle and blanket everything has disappeared. It's as if the building itself is celebrating my freedom. One of the few paintings my father hasn't sold hangs at the top of the stairs; some plain ancestor with a beauty mark on her cheek. She seems to smile at me as I pass and, foolish as it is, I smile back.

I slow my pace as I walk down the stairs. My father has emerged from his library and is bowing to Raffaello and Carina, Bianca hovering close by. Carina's face melts into a smile as soon as she sees me and her face flushes, matching the pale pink satin of her dress. She carries a basket in her gloved hands. Raffaello is elegant in his brown boots, white shirt and black velvet jacket. I feel a pang of tenderness towards my father, dressed in his shabby cloth coat.

'Laura, good day to you,' says Raffaello with a bow. 'We are both so sorry about this unpleasant business with Vincenzo.'

I drop into a curtsy. 'News spreads quickly,' I reply.

'Enough of that!' says my father. 'The past is over. Ladies, perhaps you will excuse us?' He opens his library door, gesturing for Raffaello to go through.

Carina sighs theatrically. 'Men are such gossips! Come, Laura, let's you and I sit in the courtyard.'

Raffaello kisses his wife's cheek and joins my father. Carina slips her arm through mine and we go outside. The air is thick with the sweet smell of yellow gorse and apple blossom. I take her over to the bench, shielding my eyes from the bright sun with my hands.

'Poor old Vincenzo,' she says as we sit down together, our knees touching, in a sisterly huddle. 'He'll no longer stride along the Lido being saluted to.'

'Where do you think he'll go?' I ask.

'Milan, if the rumours are true,' says Carina. 'He has a substantial fleet of ships, mostly out of port at the moment. He's lucky, really – the Doge has already impounded two of his vessels, and would have taken all of them if they'd been in Venice.'

'I feel sorry for him,' I say, remembering his grey face in the carriage.

Carina laughs, her eyes bright with astonishment. 'Really? Well, you're far more charitable than me. I think I'd throw a ball in celebration.' She squeezes my arm. 'You *are* bursting with relief, aren't you?'

Her candour is infectious, and I let my mask slip away. 'Carina, I feel like a prisoner at the gallows, with the noose round his neck, when he hears that he is to be spared after all.'

She smiles. 'Well, this better not tempt you to spend more time with the painters of Venice!'

The memory of the painter's deep eyes makes me blush.

'Of course not! But now I know what Beatrice's last days were like,' I say. 'She must have dreaded what her life was going to be like with that man as her husband and master.'

Carina takes my hand, and smiles sadly. 'At least you're free and Beatrice is at peace.'

I pray that this is true. Faustina's description of Beatrice's billowing skirts will be forever burnt on my inward eye. For a moment I want to tell Carina everything – Faustina's terrible story of the night Beatrice died, and the dark certainty that sits inside me that she was murdered. But I remember the man with the metal teeth, and decide I had better keep it all to myself.

'I've brought you a gift,' Carina smiles. She reaches into her basket, which rests on the bench beside her, and takes out two coloured headpieces, both made of tightly twisted straw – like wide-brimmed hats, except with a hole in the middle of each. One is a bright orange and the other is dark purple. She puts the purple one on her head and gracefully, with a kind of weaving movement, pulls her long silken hair through the hole. It shimmers in the sunshine like twists of copper and gold, spread out over the brim.

She passes the orange headdress to me. 'Here – one of Venice's great beauty secrets,' she confides. 'Look, the colour goes perfectly with your dress.'

'What does it do?' I wonder.

'It's just a little trickery to keep your hair golden,' she laughs.

She helps to fit it on top of my head and I pull my hair

through just as she has done. I feel her fingers arranging and spreading my locks. 'There. All you need to do is sit out like this every day and let the sun do its work. A bit of lemon juice will help lighten the colour, as well.'

'Thank you,' I say. 'You've no idea how much your kindness means to me. I adore Faustina, but it's so lovely to have someone my own age to talk to. Especially now. Father's in a crisis.'

'Men always are,' says Carina. 'The higher they climb up the tree of power, the weaker the branches become.'

I can imagine her words coming from Allegreza.

Loud, angry shouts burst from the house and we both sit up straight. It's my father's voice, and then Raffaello's. I can't make out any words until my father bellows 'Soon!' I look to Carina and see that her face has darkened. She tosses her head-dress into her basket, stands up, and strides towards the house.

'What's happening?' I ask, hurrying after her, my own head-dress in my hand.

'Oh, I'm sure it's nothing important,' Carina says, though her face is still stern and serious. 'In any case, it's best to ignore the skirmishes of male affairs.'

The door to the palazzo flies open. Raffaello bolts out like an enraged bull. He stamps down the steps towards us, seizing Carina's arm. 'Come. We're going.'

Carina pulls herself free and takes his hand instead. As he almost yanks her down the path, she calls to me over her shoulder. 'I'll see you soon – very soon.'

'Goodbye!' I reply. But she and Raffaello are already through the gate.

I drift back inside. The cool of the hall seems chilly, and the lurking darkness makes me feel blind after the warmth of the sun.

My father sits in his library, slumped and deflated. His elbows rest on the desk and he combs his fingers through his limp hair.

'Father, are you all right? What happened?'

He begins to talk, but for a little while, I'm not sure he even knows I'm there.

'First Vincenzo, and now that *snake* Raffaello . . . Is there a conspiracy to keep me from the halls of power?' He looks up and waves me away as if there's an insect pestering him. 'Anyway, it's none of your concern.'

'But I thought you and Raffaello were friends.'

My father gives a short, joyless laugh. 'Laura, there are no friends in Venice. Leave me alone.'

19

My father spends the morning striding around the house, his boots squeaking and stamping on the floor. I eat alone, while he takes his meal in the library. I peek in to see if he wants anything and he's scribbling a letter. There is a pile of them on his desk, scrolled and sealed with red wax. He asks me to call for Bianca and he gives her the letters, despatching her hither and thither across the city. 'I'm not a messenger,' she grumbles as she flounces past me and out into the streets.

He corners me in the salon, where I'm continuing my mother's book of love poems.

'Right,' he says. 'This is what's going to happen now. You're to get to know Paulina.'

'I know her already, Father.'

'Well, you're to get to know her better. If I'm right, and I *do* have a nose for these things, she's soon to be married into a powerful family. God knows how, as the uncle who keeps her is an imbecile. Do you understand how important it is for us to foster such connections, especially now?'

'Yes, Father.'

'Good. I've arranged for you to meet her this afternoon. At the Piazza della Angela.'

He makes it sound like a business meeting, but the thought of seeing Paulina again, and of getting away from the tense atmosphere of the palazzo, is a welcome one. There's much to tell her.

I put down my book and kiss his rough cheek. 'Thank you, Father.'

He stares at me, seeming surprised by my gesture. 'Good,' he says. 'Don't let me down.'

'Mother Mary! Can't you keep it still?' Faustina grumbles as she topples into the wobbling gondola. Both the gondolier and I catch her hands, helping her to her seat. She rearranges her skirts and looks about her, her eyes bright in her kind old face. 'What a treat it is to be on the canals today.'

The water is crowded with gondolas and tiny sail boats. Crowds throng along the lanes and bridges, chattering like gaudy birds. Our gondolier arranges a shady awning over us, then pushes his pole down and eases away from the bank.

The sun grins down at the world like a menacing rival, but I am cool in the shade. I trail my fingers in the water as our gondolier threads his way towards the south-western shore. Another boatman calls across a challenge to a race and our gondolier grins at us. 'This man questions my skill. If I lose, you will travel for free.'

I agree, before Faustina can object, and the contest begins. Lifting his pole in and out of the water with swift, smooth movements, our boat cleaves the canal. Though a few splashes of water sprinkle over us, we overtake the other gondola, and even Faustina giggles like a young girl behind my fan.

The gondolier pulls up by a side canal and helps us out. I pay him, and add a tip for his success. From there, we walk to Piazza della Angela. The square is edged by tall, crumbling pink houses, and dotted with people selling fruit and sugared almonds. Men and women walk in the sunshine, buying treats and laughing. And right in the middle, twirling a parasol, is Paulina. Her curly black hair tumbles down her back. Her blue dress has a tight bodice, with a skirt that flares with flashes of pale yellow.

Faustina kisses me on both cheeks. 'Enjoy yourself, and forget about these last few days. Remember, you're to come home before supper – don't make me worry about you.'

'I won't,' I say, and Faustina moves off among the crowd.

Paulina smiles and waves when she notices me approaching.

'How good it is to see you,' she says, taking my arm. She leads me into a narrow lane that seems half asleep. 'Oh, Laura, I was so relieved to hear your news!'

She spins me around so our skirts fly out in a swirl of colour. Our laughter echoes against the stooping stone walls.

'Everything seems so different now I'm free of him,' I say. The heels of our silk shoes tap against the cobbles.

'And now the *real* search for a husband begins,' she says.

I feel my cheeks reddening. 'That isn't what I meant.'

'But it's what will surely follow,' she replies.

The street widens and market stalls crowd each other on either side. The people here are poor, their clothes worn and dirty, but their faces are happy as they joke and jostle each other, turning pigs on spits and grilling chops and steaks. The smell of food, bubbling and roasting, is thick in the air. A young man selling roast chickens raises his cap at me, and I smile.

'Anyway,' I say, 'my father tells me that you've got some news of your own.'

Paulina's face lights up. 'Men! They know our affairs before we know them ourselves!'

'So is it true?'

She nods, and steps aside as a man carrying a tray of small cups high over his head darts past. From her skipping feet and the way her eyes shine, I know that she's far happier about her upcoming marriage than I was.

'Well,' I continue. 'Are you going to tell me who he is?'

She twirls her parasol as we pass into another lane, where a cheering crowd is gathered around street performers. 'Oh, Laura, it's a love match! It's what we all deserve. I pray that you too will find the same happiness. I'm sure you will.'

We move to the front of the crowd and see a street dancer with bells on his costume, twisting himself in knots. The rhythm of the bells is enchanting, and we join the others in clapping our hands in time. Through the laughing faces I see a tall man at the edge of the crowd, with a wide black hat that casts a shadow on his face. The angle of that face is different from the throngs around him. He seems to be looking at us rather than the dancer.

I nudge Paulina and point at him. 'Is that someone you know?' But he pushes his way from the crowd and disappears.

'Where?' she asks.

'A man in a black hat,' I say. 'He was watching us.'

Paulina smiles. 'You should get used to that,' she said. 'When you look as fine as you, men are bound to stare.'

The acrobatic display comes to an end, and people toss coins into the gaudy coloured hat proffered by the performer. When a red-dressed young woman in front of me has made her donation, I take a coin from my velvet purse and follow suit.

'Thank you, ladies,' the performer says.

The young woman in red turns and stares, her eyes moving up and down Paulina. She nudges her companion and they snigger behind their open fans.

Paulina sighs crossly, then takes my arm and leads me away. 'Ignore them,' she says.

'Do you know that girl?' I ask, when we've rounded the next corner.

'My uncle used to work for her father,' she says. 'She looks down on my family. Though she won't be so insolent when I'm married. Then no woman will be able to look down on me. Even the Segreta's power won't reach high enough to bring me down.'

My body tenses. I can feel the colour drain from my face and I pretend to look at a passing carriage, hoping Paulina won't notice.

'The Segreta?' I speak as calmly as I am able, then move my hand surreptitiously behind my back to hide the small bandage from my initiation ceremony. It's silly, of course. She couldn't know.

'That's one name they use,' says Paulina. 'Some call them the Society of Secrets, or the Hidden Women. Part of the appeal is the silly names, I expect.'

'Appeal of what?' I ask carefully.

She tightens her arm around mine, drawing me close and lowering her voice conspiratorially. 'It's a group of Venetian women. My sister told me about them when I was small. No one knows who belongs to the Segreta, or what they really do. My sister says they get rid of people.'

I feel a bead of sweat trickle along my spine.

Paulina laughs. 'Don't look so serious! Probably they just gossip about men and money and gowns, like all the other women of Venice.' She takes out her fan and beats the air, making her dark curls flutter. 'It's too hot; let's go into the cathedral.'

I've lost my bearings, but she leads me across a few lanes and canals, and we emerge into the glinting St Mark's Square. The piazza is dominated by the silvery domes and intricate spires of the cathedral. Before it stands the bell tower, a red-orange square brick column, casting a shadow eastwards over the Doge's palazzo. The salty smell of the sea wafts up from St Mark's Canal and gulls wheel overhead. As we walk towards the cathedral entrance, I glance around. Despite the heat, there's a chill at my back, an eerie breeze that doesn't belong to a day like this. The man in the black hat is there again. He halts and I lose sight of him among the crowd.

We step from the furnace of the Venetian day into the cool blackness of St Mark's interior. The air is like having a sweet, cool bath of oils, incense and holiness. If I close my eyes I could be back in the convent again. A statue of Jesus stretches over the crucifix, the agony of a world of sinners on his poor bleeding face. Little candles dance in the side chapel, where a statue of Our Lady stoops in divine humility. The great domed ceiling collects and swells the whisper of the worshippers.

Beatrice used to tell me that in St Mark's Cathedral every visitor has the same expression on his face. Dreamy but watchful, prayerful but alert – I see it on the faces of those here today. Knots of old women kneel in worship close to the altar, running rosary beads through their fingers. A friar bustles around the altar, busy and official. A woman in a yellow cape comes in after Paulina and me, glancing towards us with liquid-brown eyes that remind me of a young deer. As she kneels facing the altar one of the old women shifts away, scowling.

Paulina and I genuflect at the altar. We dip our fingers in holy water and bless ourselves. These old rituals soothe me with the rhythms of my past. God is watching, and I wonder if He recognizes me now, no longer the little brown-clad novice I was.

'There's something that I want you to see,' Paulina whispers.

I follow her to the south-eastern end of the cathedral, from where covered passages run to the Doge's palazzo. An ivory screen carved with scenes of Christ's miracles has been folded back to reveal two slightly elevated sarcophagi, one of purple-brown porphyry, the other polished black marble. They lie side by side, equal in length.

'Who were they?' I ask. My words are hushed, but they seem to violate the lingering tragedy suspended over the two tombs.

'You remember the couple whom the Doge sent away from the ball – the man and wife in black?'

Carina's parents.

'Julius de Ferrara and his wife,' I say.

'That's right. Well, this is the cause.' She gestured towards the sarcophagi. 'These boys were the doomed sons of powerful foes. I've never understood why they buried them next to each other like this – so the families could spit hatred across the tombs, I suppose. The de Ferraras lost their only son. At least the Doge and his wife still have their second boy, Nicolo.'

She smiles to herself and her eyes flick towards me, but I am thinking of Carina. I now understand the thread of toughness coiled beneath her golden exterior – she is mourning her poor brother.

Paulina continues. 'The Doge and his wife, the Duchess Besina – their son who lies here was called Roberto.' She nods towards the porphyry tomb. 'He was only eleven. The de Ferraras declared a vendetta after the Doge executed their son, Carlo, for treason. They found out that Carlo was innocent, so they took the life of the Doge's boy in recompense. He was stabbed right through the heart. They say the knife came out the other side of him.'

'How could anyone do such a thing to a boy?'

Paulina shakes her head. 'It's easy enough to hire a man at the docks to kill, they say. A few pieces of silver – it doesn't buy absolution, but it saves getting blood on your own hands.'

Is it so easy? I wonder. I think of the man who terrified Faustina that night. Did someone pay him to kill my sister?

I shake my head. 'What wasted lives.'

'In a way their parents' lives have been wasted too, considering how they've been at each others' throats ever since,' she replies. 'Carina is sick of it all. She doesn't want anything to do with it. I sometimes wonder if that's why she married Raffaello – to escape her family.'

I can't help imagining the young skeletons contained behind these deathly decorations. I move between them to where a bank of candles flicker. I take a long taper and light two more, one for each boy, and then a third for Beatrice. I go back to stand by Paulina, and she bows her head and crosses herself.

'Listen, Laura,' she says, casting a furtive glance around. 'I've something to tell you.'

She draws me by the elbow away from the tombs, and I feel the excitement in her touch. I am to learn another secret.

'What is it?' I ask.

Her face lifts. Her eyes sparkle. 'I've told you all this because . . . because I may become a part of it.'

'Part of this vendetta?'

'Oh, no! Not like that . . . Remember I told you that the Doge has a second son – poor Roberto's younger brother – called Nicolo?'

I nod, suddenly understanding where her story will lead.

'Well, guess whose name Nicolo has carved into the cypress tree at the back of the Doge's palace? Go on, guess!'

I rest my chin in my hands, screwing up my face in pretend thought. 'Faustina?'

Tendrils of joy seem to spread through her. She gives me a playful shove then presses her palms to her breast.

'Mine!' she cries. 'I'm almost sure to be married to him!'

A couple of the old women turn from their prayers, staring at us scoldingly.

I kiss her cheeks, and in a lower voice say, 'I'm so happy for you. To marry someone you love, and to think, Nicolo might even be elected as Doge one day!'

'He's wonderful!' she says. 'I would love him if he didn't have a penny to his name. So many girls have tried to get his attention, but he says his heart belongs to me. I think he's going to propose at Count Raffaello's hunting party this weekend. Have you been invited?'

My heart sinks. After my father's argument with Raffaello, of course I'm not invited. 'I don't know,' I mutter.

'Oh,' she says, squeezing my hand, 'I'm sure Carina will want you there. Laura, I'm so happy to have you here again. I've been keeping Nicolo a secret for so long, but I just had to tell you.'

We walk underneath the echoing domes back to the grand entrance.

'And don't you worry,' she adds. 'We're sure to find a match for you soon as well!'

I smile, though inwardly I think that I should be grateful to have escaped marriage for now. I can't imagine that I would ever feel a joy like that on Paulina's face.

When we slip out into St Mark's Square, squinting in the sunshine, I spot the woman in the yellow cape. As we pass, she holds her hand out.

'Spare a poor sinner the price of bread, my ladies,' she murmurs. 'God bless you. God bless you.'

There's something fragile in her brown eyes that makes me rummage in my purse.

'You shouldn't encourage beggars, Laura,' Paulina chides under her breath.

'I was a nun, once,' I remind her. 'Tending to the needy was the only holy act I saw in that convent.'

'Thank you, merciful girl,' says the woman. She smiles at me, dimples creasing her tanned cheeks. 'Heaven reward you.'

I press the coins into her palm. But suddenly the noise of the piazza, of Paulina's urges to move on, fade into silence and my world narrows to one point – the ring of twisted gold on the beggar woman's finger.

It's my sister's ring.

My purse tumbles from my grasp. All its contents scatter, clatter and chime like little bells on the ground.

'Laura!' cries Paulina, stooping to scoop them up.

But I ignore her. I feel a rush of bitterness rising inside my throat.

'Where did you get that ring?'

Her smile has gone.

She steps away but I seize her wrist.

'Leave me be,' she mutters, struggling and pulling away from me. I snatch at her yellow cape. The edges of her face are haggard, older than the supple strength of her young body. Her brown eyes are hurt, but ferocity lurks there too. As we tussle, her cape loosens, showing a blue silk gown. It's torn and shabby, and reveals the curves of her breasts and the skin on her belly. She's not just a beggar. She's one of the Venetian women of the night.

'Why are you wearing my sister's ring?' I cry, my voice high and hysterical. 'What do you know about Beatrice?'

She jerks out of my clutches, and backs away, pointing the ringed finger at me. 'Keep away!'

The crowd that has gathered to stare hurry back to let her pass, as if she might draw a knife from the tarnished silk of her bosom. She disappears into the dark alleys and waterways, the panels of her cape flapping behind her like the wings of a giant bird.

20

'I shouldn't have indulged myself like that,' frets Paulina. 'Chattering on about Nicolo, while you're still grieving for dear Beatrice. Oh Laura, forgive me.'

I'm hardly listening to her as our gondola slowly takes us away from the drama, back towards my father's house.

'Why has that woman got my sister's ring?' I wonder, knowing that Paulina can't possibly give me an answer.

'Laura, are you absolutely sure it was Beatrice's?' She takes my hand and looks at my own ring. 'It's not that unusual a design. There must be hundreds of rings that look just like this. I don't want to see you so upset for nothing.'

She speaks softly to me, her face gentle and concerned. I don't know how to answer her.

We step off the boat and Paulina insists on walking me back to the palazzo.

'Really, there's no need,' I say. 'I'm sure you have so many things to do.'

'Don't be silly,' she says.

We stop talking after that. She doesn't believe that the beggar woman was wearing Beatrice's ring. Why should she? She hasn't gazed at its twin every day for four years. Though her arm is threaded through mine what happened in St Mark's Square separates us. By the time we get to the front door, she might as well be looking down on me from the top of a mountain, so great is the distance between us.

My father quickly bids Paulina farewell, pulls me inside and closes the door. Through the tall glass panel I see her trotting down to the gate. She swings her closed fan around so that it looks like a coloured ball spinning in her hand.

My father's face darkens. 'What took you so long?' my father asks. 'Bianca and Faustina are waiting upstairs. Hurry!'

'But Father, what –?'

'Look at the state of your clothes,' he interrupts. I look down and see that my silk shoes and the hem of my orange gown are smeared with the dust of the Venetian streets. 'Go!'

Confused, I stumble up to my room. Faustina and Bianca are laying out a cream dress with gold edging on the bed. Bianca sees my filthy shoes and lets out a little wail.

Faustina pulls me to her and goes to work on unfastening my dress.

'Paulina and I were at St Mark's,' I tell her. 'I saw a woman there – a prostitute. She was wearing my sister's ring, Faustina. I'm sure of it.'

Her hands still, and in a whisper that Bianca can't hear, she says, 'Sweetheart, how could that be possible?'

It's like Paulina all over again. 'I know what I saw.'

She puts her palm to my forehead. 'You're hot,' she murmurs. 'It's this weather. What happened to Beatrice is terrible – appalling. You must try not to upset yourself like this.'

She finishes unhooking my dress and it slides to the floor. I step out of it, tears of frustration stinging my eyes. I want to say more, but with Bianca here it's difficult.

'What are we getting ready for?' I ask.

'The Doge,' Bianca says, pouring drops of rosewater into the washbowl. 'He's invited your father to visit him this evening.'

I'm stunned. 'The Doge? Of Venice?'

'No, the Doge of the Moon,' says Faustina with a smile.

She holds back my hair while Bianca wrings a cloth in a basin of steaming water, sponging it over my face. They flap and scramble around me like doves fighting in a tree. They wash my hair, and enhance the natural waves with ivory tongs that tug at my scalp. They slip the creamy dress over my head and tighten it to my waist, and put a golden chain around my neck. My hair dries in curls around my face and on my shoulders. The skin of my face is untouched, but for my lips they prepare a mix of crushed carmine beetles and henna. When they hold up the mirror, there's a glow coming from me that doesn't reveal the jumble of things that I'm thinking. I look like a privileged woman, young and carefree, with nothing to worry about but keeping my velvet slippers clean.

The Doge's face surveys the room while the Duchess swishes among the guests. We're in a smaller, more intimate chamber than where the ball took place, but it is no less ornate or impressive. Huge tapestries of war and feasting hang on each wall, vignettes from ancient times. I recognize some of them from my mother's books. Here Aeneas flees Troy with his father on his back and young Ascanius clutching his hand. There the wandering hero presents himself before Dido, Queen of Carthage. Every inch of each of the broad tables around which people move is covered in dishes – spiralling patterns of delicate bread, fish and Tuscan meats. A whole suckling pig eyes me from the centre of one table. Olives, green and purple-black, glisten in little terracotta pots. The men pick them up with their fingers and toss them into their mouths as if they're devouring prey. The women use tiny silver forks and napkins, taking prim little nibbles between snippets of conversation. Even the servants are glorious in white and deep green.

The Doge's wife with her black and gold fan seems to radiate good health, even more so than those who are younger and smoother than her. She smiles and touches people's elbows when she's talking to them. From time to time she glances back at her husband. She catches my eye and nods at me. I curtsy, wondering if she could guess that of all the people in this room, I am the one who is a traitor to the Doge's secret.

I take a plump green olive from the platter a servant offers me. Across the room I see Allegreza, in a black gown with white slashes on the skirt, black feathers in her hair. She's speaking intently to a group of older women. I imagine that she's whispering the Doge's secret to them, then they will whisper it to others until it spreads like the plague itself into the homes and businesses and boats and barges of our city.

'Laura, stand up straight,' warns my father.

The Doge is approaching us. The rich purple of his doublet gleams in the candlelight.

I feel my cheeks redden. The olive pit is still in my mouth. I put my hand to my lips, pressing the stone into my palm, and slip it inside my velvet purse. I feel clumsy, unable to navigate the narrow straits of polite society. I'm sure that I'll never learn the language of the Venetian party, so full of incomprehensible nuances, glances, mutters, postures and barbs.

'Your Grace,' says my father with a deep bow. I curtsy beside him.

'Antonio, Laura. So glad, so glad. Such a dreadful business with Vincenzo. Who would have thought?'

'Yes, thank you, Your Grace,' my father says with another bow. 'I'm eternally grateful to you for expediting that matter so speedily on everyone's behalf.'

'No need,' says the Doge. He holds his hand up and shakes his head slightly. His eyes pass to me, and he stares for a little longer than feels comfortable. I wonder for a brief, awful second if he's trying to place me, to remember where he's seen me before. But then he moves on into the crowd.

'God damn me altogether!' my father hisses. His fists are clenched. 'I'm done for.'

'But the Doge was friendly to us.'

'Men in the Doge's favour get two or three minutes of conversation with him. How long did he stand with us for? It can't have been more than a few seconds. Confound it. And you? You just stood there like a puppet, waiting for me to pull the strings.'

Anger stirs beneath the cream silk of my bodice. 'And what did you want me to say?'

He throws his hands wide. 'It wouldn't have mattered *what* you said, if only you'd said something. Changed the subject. Talked about the weather. Been charming and witty like your sister always used to be.'

I want to snap at him – tell him I can't help it if he feels the wrong daughter died. But my father holds my future in his hands and I don't dare. I mumble an apology and walk away from him through the throng.

Allegreza moves towards me. I pretend not to have noticed her, and quicken my pace. What could she want from me? I've exchanged my secret for what the Segreta did to Vincenzo, and now I want nothing more to do with them. Their power frightens me.

But Allegreza tracks me across the room, like a spider closing in on a fly. She places a cool hand on my arm.

'Please don't,' I say, trying to pull away.

She tightens her grip, her eyebrows arched above her almond eyes. 'Why, don't you know me, child?'

I can't tell if she means to be reproachful or to tease.

I shake my head. 'I'm sorry, I . . . I'll always be grateful. But I've paid you for it, so please, will you leave me alone?'

She pulls me towards her and whispers quickly. There's no escape in her words.

'I can't do that, Laura. When you accepted our help you became bound to us. We're gathering at the monastery tomorrow night. You will be there. A boat will await you – look for the key.'

With a rustle of silk she drops my arm and sweeps away.

The mark on my hand has almost healed, but I see now it isn't inconsequential at all.

I remember what I learned in the convent: the fee is never paid.

21

I slip down a narrow staircase, my hand pressed to my chest to calm my breathing, out to a formal garden. A cluster of lanterns on a low wall light up clipped trees and shrubs in ordered lines and circles. Little stone paths thread through them, bordered with crowds of tiny coloured blossoms. I take a deep breath of the cool night air. It feels good to get out of the palace with its cloying atmosphere of ambition and intrigue.

The garden wall slopes down to St Mark's Basin – the stretch of water that laps up against the Doge's palace. I hold my skirts in one hand, raising the hem so I can follow the wall to the waterfront, but suddenly spot a figure silhouetted against the night sky. There's a box of charcoal by his side, and from the movements of his arm I can tell that he is sketching.

The painter.

He seems so lost in his work that he doesn't notice my presence.

'Hello,' I say.

He starts, and turns towards me. His red mouth breaks into a smile and his dark eyes shine. He scrambles to his feet.

'Hello again,' he says.

'Please, don't get up.'

He settles back down and pats the space next to him. I hold up my dress and sit beside him, my legs curled under me.

'My father and I are here at the Doge's party,' I explain.

'That's a shame,' he says. 'I thought you'd come just to hunt me down.'

I laugh, and perhaps it's the light, or my imagination, but his cheeks seem warm with colour.

He picks up a stick of charcoal. In his lap is a board with a piece of parchment fixed to it. He makes quick strokes over the surface.

'What are you drawing?' I ask.

He tilts the board towards me. It's the scene I can see stretched out before us – the water, and the low buildings of Giudecca Island stretched across the horizon. I'm amazed that from just a few lines, I can sense the cool of the canal and the solid stone of the buildings.

'It's perfect,' I murmur.

He smiles. 'It'll never be that.'

He rummages through the box of charcoal and selects a fine, delicate piece. In the foreground of the scene he sketches a slick, black gondola. He adds a stooped gondolier, dragging his pole through the water, and then a seated passenger – a woman. The slant of her shoulders, the shape of her neck and the way her eyes are downcast, are instantly familiar.

'It's me!' I gasp. Pleasure flushes through me. 'I've never been in a picture before.'

'I'd like to make a proper picture of you one day – a painting, in oils.'

He holds my gaze. His dark eyes seem to be searching for something within my own so intently that I'm forced to look away, down at my dress. I realize I must look just like my image in his drawing.

'But for now, this one needs a name,' he says. '*Giudecca at Night, with Signorina . . .?*'

'Laura.'

He repeats my name, seeming to linger over the word. 'I'm Giacomo.'

St Mark's bell tower chimes at the hour. The sound ripples across the churches throughout the city.

Eleven. I should be back inside. My father will wonder where I am.

I smile. 'I must go.'

'Of course,' he says.

He helps me to my feet and we stand there, not moving for a while. He doesn't take his eyes off my face. I murmur good-bye and walk back through the gardens. As I go, I hope that he's standing there, looking at me still.

Later that night my father and I sit in the dining room. He growls to himself as he opens another bottle from the cellar, pouring the ruby-red wine into his goblet with a shaking hand. Bianca attends us, her hair already woven into a long plait for the night. She tries to put a cork in the bottle, but he swats her away.

He points at me. 'You're going to have to start cooperating. Make sure Paulina introduces you to more of her circle. Someone told me she'll marry the Doge's son.'

'Yes, father. She and I had talked of it today.'

'Well, what's the news?' he asks, leaning towards me as if my face has something written on it. His voice is slurred and his breath soured by drink.

'She talked about the hunt Raffaello and Carina are hosting.'

I'm instantly sorry I've mentioned it. He downs the contents of his goblet, then flings it on the floor. It smashes into a puddle of dregs and splinters of glass.

I see Bianca shake her head crossly. There's a faint knock on the door and she slips from the room.

'That bloody hunt!' he shouts. 'The whole of Venice is going and we're not even on the spectator list! You know Beatrice and I went last year? It's where she first met Vincenzo. Oh, if I was only on the Grand Council. How everything is so changed. And you!' He stands up, his fists digging into the table. 'If I don't find another husband for you, you'll just have to go back to the convent! So it's up to you – if you can't secure a man through Paulina, I can't afford to keep you.'

His words sting, but I'm too weary and it's late in the evening for an argument.

Bianca reappears at the dining-room door.

'Excuse me, master,' she says. 'There's a message for you. Delivered earlier.' She holds out a creamy scroll. 'I forgot to give it . . .'

My father snatches it and breaks the wax seal.

It's an invitation to the hunt. Both our names are painted on to the parchment in black ink.

My father jumps up, tipping over his chair. His scowl has changed into a smile, and he takes me by the hands and swings me round.

'The della Scalas are still a force to be reckoned with!' he laughs. 'Perhaps we are not lost after all.'

It's like living with two different people. One moment he's dour, critical, frowning. The next he's frantic, excitable, laughing. I don't know which version of him is worse.

He reaches for the wine bottle, taking another goblet from the shelves along the wall. As he pours another drink, Bianca beckons me with her finger.

'There's a messenger here now,' she whispers. 'That's what made me think of the invitation. The message is for you. He says he's to give it to you himself.'

My skin prickles with excitement. A messenger for me? At this hour? I return to the table. 'Father, it's very late. I think I'll go to bed.'

He raises his goblet to me. 'Yes, of course, excellent girl. I'll be turning in myself soon.'

I suspect I'll find him slumped over the table in the morning, the bottle empty.

Bianca and I rush out of the room.

'Where? Where is he?' I don't even try to hide the delight that has risen to the surface of me.

'I told him to wait in the courtyard, by the bench,' says Bianca.

We run through the hall and I fling open the front door.

Bianca touches my shoulder. 'I'll be just here. Shout if you need me.'

I give her a grateful smile and run through the courtyard. I'm expecting to see a dark-haired man with an olive-tinted face, paint splashed over his clothes. The smell of lemon balm kisses the air. My hurrying steps startle a cat, which lets out a snide mew. Then I see him, a figure by the bench, under the shadows of the cypress tree.

It's not who I expect. I haven't seen this man before.

'Oh,' I say. I try to regain my poise. 'Hello.'

'Signorina,' the man replies with a bow, 'my name is Mathieu.' His accent isn't one I've heard before. I wonder if he's from the south, from Naples, perhaps. He's my father's age, with kindly lines that crinkle around his eyes. He takes something out of the pocket of his jacket.

'I'm Giacomo's servant. My master wishes me to tell you that you're in his thoughts. He bids me pass this token of his regard to you.'

He holds a little package in the palm of his hand. It's wrapped in soft orange silk. I pull the twine that holds it together, and open it to reveal a wooden bird – a swift, with its wings outstretched – beautifully carved, perfectly finished. It makes me smile.

'Mathieu, thank you,' I say. 'And please pass on my gratitude to Signor Giacomo.'

'Of course,' he says and lowers his head in a little shallow bow. He half turns to go, then grins. 'You're just as he described you, Signorina.'

I wonder what he means as he walks past the low wall and through my father's gates, with a purposeful untroubled stride.

I slip back into the house. I hear my father snoring in the dining room and fetch one of the furs lying in the salon, spreading it over his shoulders.

But though I'm desperately tired I can't sleep, no matter

how much I remember Faustina dabbing invisible honey on my eyelids. I lie curled on my side, holding Giacomo's carved wooden gift between my fingers, turning it over and imagining his own fingers doing the same. My body quivers and I try to quiet my thoughts. I mustn't think about a painter boy in this way. It's quite wrong.

22

The following night I sit by my window, watching the shadows move around the courtyard as I wait for the house to fall silent. I calculate that I have almost four hours before the first clues of morning will thread their whispers around the night clouds. I make a decision. I have to do as Allegreza said. If their power is as great as the swiftness of Vincenzo's departure suggests, then the Segreta might be helpful in unlocking the other secret that plagues me. Murders are built on secrets, after all. A motive lurks in the mind of a killer until it is uncovered: a debt that can't be paid, an adulterous affair, jealousy that blossoms into a poisonous flower of hatred. If I can find the reason my sister was killed, then perhaps it will lead me to her killer.

I get up, slip into a green linen day dress and throw my cape over my shoulders. I pull out my mask from its secret place in my bottom drawer, tuck it into the deep silk pocket of my cape, and head out into the night.

There are several boats in the harbour, their sailors sitting on the jetties, chattering in low voices. But one boat catches my attention, for on its hull is sketched the outline of a key.

When its pilot sees me he stands upright and alert. I pass the other vessels to his.

'Can you take me to San Michele?' I ask, offering a coin. Despite our penury, my father has given me a small allowance.

The boatman waves it away with his hand. 'It would be my pleasure,' he says.

It feels like I've made this journey a thousand times. Perhaps that's how often I've followed the wake of this crossing in my head.

When the boat slides to a halt, I thank the boatman and step out once again on to the chequered courtyard. Again the friar emerges; he nods in silent greeting and I follow him into the monastery. His sandalled feet are silent but my footsteps ring like some lone person clapping in the dark.

We wind through the maze of corridors and up the spiral stairs. As we near the meeting room I put on the shimmering white disguise. The friar steps aside and I see them all gathered, just as they were before. The woman in the fox mask is first to notice me.

'Ah, it's the little swan,' she says.

Allegreza stands in the centre of the group in her owl mask, but it's a different woman who beckons me forward.

'Welcome.' Her mask is shaped like a black cat's face, studded with pieces of jet. Her entire outfit is black, from the top of her head to her dark shoes. She wears long black gloves and her white hair is laced with a black satin ribbon. 'You shouldn't be nervous, child, for here we are your friends.'

I recognize her voice at once, and the face behind the mask, though invisible, forms out of my memory. It's Grazia, Carina's mother: the woman who, with her husband, was ousted from the Doge's party. The woman whose dead son lies interred in St Mark's.

'I saw you,' I say. 'At the Doge's palace.'

I worry that I've said the wrong thing, but if I've offended her, she doesn't betray any displeasure.

'There are some things we can't forget,' she says. 'Our children paid a high price – too high for ones so young.'

'I'm sorry for your loss.'

'Thank you,' she says. 'But your own grief is even fresher.'

She puts her warm hand on mine.

The Segreta gather in a loose semicircle, facing me. Grazia nods. Do they expect me to speak?

'I want to thank you,' I manage. 'You engineered my freedom, and for that I'm . . .'

The women murmur to each other. Their eyes glare at me, and they're like a flock of hostile birds, clicking and alert. Some put their hands up to their ears in the way I remember the nuns doing at the convent when they heard anything they thought they shouldn't.

Allegreza holds up her hand. 'Silence! Don't say another word.'

'I don't understand. Vincenzo . . .'

She steps towards me. Her voice is low but not unkind. 'Laura, we thought you understood. No one ever discusses what the Society does, or implies that it is responsible for any actions or events that unfold in Venice. It's dangerous to link us to anything. There are cracks in every wall in this city. There are windows and eaves and gaps through which rumours might escape. Do you understand? This is for everyone's protection, including yours.'

'I'm sorry. I didn't realize.'

'There's something else you need to do for us, Laura,' she says.

I shake my head. 'I have no more secrets.'

'It's not that,' she says. 'We need you to recruit a trusting heart to the Segreta. Bring us someone who will join us.'

I stare at her, amazed. 'But how can I possibly do that? I'm not even allowed to speak of your existence.'

The women laugh and bob their heads behind their rustling masks. I feel myself blush beneath my own, but still have no idea how to accomplish what they ask.

'I managed with you,' says Allegreza, 'and so you shall find a way. Because you're a clever girl, and you have a strength inside that you have only just begun to use.'

'And if I fail?' I ask quietly.

No one answers, and my mind fills their silence with a dozen threats. Their power throbs and fills the chamber. They brought down a member of the Grand Council; what's a convent girl to them?

A distant bell chimes and the meeting breaks up. We process in silence back through the monastery. Grazia glides at my side. Several boats have gathered by the chequered floor. Our oarsmen take us back to the main island as the sky lightens, little boats fanning off in all directions.

As I hold on to the rocking edge of the boat I'm struck by another truth. Just as the Segreta pulled their strings and removed Vincenzo, now they're manipulating me.

23

'I can't wait to get in the saddle again!' my father declares. 'I only hope they don't give me some old nag.'

He's said the same thing, or a close variation, three times already that morning. I'm starting to feel sorry for the horse. The brevity of our conversation with the Doge, and the social exile it implied, seem to be forgotten.

Depending on the way the light falls upon it, my dress shimmers as light as a pale new violet, or as dark as a rich amethyst. I'm grateful for my broad hat as we cross to the mainland of the Veneto on a sailing barge, one of a small fleet that has been sent by our hosts. The sun pours down, bright but merciless, making the faces of the young even more youthful, and the faces of the old, more aged. Once we land on the other side, we are brought by simple carriage to Raffaello and Carina's hunting lodge on the banks of a small lake. It's a resplendent place, tall and turreted, and the gates receive us like the open arms of a grand relative. The big news, and I hear it from at least three mouths, is that the Doge himself hasn't been able to come, due to illness. I wonder, guiltily, if it's the illness I couldn't keep secret. No one seems unhappy by his absence – if anything, the mood lifts at the thought of being unsupervised, like boys in a schoolroom without a tutor.

Gloved fingers are gripped by manly hands as ladies are greeted. Men's cheeks are brushed with puckered lips. Ribbons of blue and yellow flap festively from every tree and pillar, and seem to grow so that by the time we're at the door, they flop gigantically, great wreaths of fabric largesse, hanging in celebration of the noble family to whom these colours belong.

My father can't stop smiling. It looks like he has a cramp in his face. He wears his hunting gear, faded and thinning in places, but good enough, he resolved last night, for another outing.

We arrive just in time. Men in brocade coats, black trousers and big-buckled boots are rounding everyone up, getting ready for the hunt. Two men rake a wide dusty tree-lined path. The horses have purpose in their eyes. Smoky air tumbles from their nostrils and soft thuds echo as they hit the ground with their hooves, snorting impatiently. One of them tosses its head in agitation. I reach out to it and put my hand on its long nose.

'*Calma*,' I whisper.

It's then that I feel someone else's hand on my own shoulder and I jump. Giacomo stands right beside me. I breathe in sharp and full. He smells like paint and apples. He smiles in his soft clothes: his black cotton trousers, sandals that show his toes.

'Hello, you,' he whispers, and I turn to him, his face right next to mine.

'You're here,' I say. It's hard to tear my eyes away from his face, but I must in case anyone is watching. 'I mean, I didn't expect it.'

Giacomo pats the horse's back, and makes comforting little humming, clicking noises to soothe it. 'I've been commissioned to sketch the hunting party and I'm behind on it already. Too many distractions.'

'Is that what I am?' I ask.

'A welcome distraction,' he says.

'Thank you for your gift,' I whisper. 'It was kind of you, but . . .' I'm suddenly aware that we're standing very close. He's even taller than I remember. I see my father, between handshakes, casting his glance around.

'But what?' he asks.

'Well, I just think it would be better if you didn't send me anything like that again. My father would not take kindly . . .'

He looks crestfallen. 'Very well, Laura.'

'It's not that I didn't like it,' I add hurriedly. 'It was beautiful, it's just . . .'

'I'd better go,' he says. He bows his head and backs away from me, and then he turns and disappears into the bustle of servants, noblemen, stable boys and silk-dressed ladies. I watch his loose white shirt and his black curls weaving through the crowd.

I rummage fiercely in my velvet bag for my fan. I open it in front of me. It's purple too, with silver threads stitched around each boned section. I move it over my face to cool my skin.

Carina emerges from the door of the lodge in a yellow dress. Raffaello holds her arm, and the guests flock to the hosts. Men drink wine from silver goblets. Some of the hunters have already started to clamber up on to the horses. Coloured birds screech in the trees, heralding the dramatic departure of the hunt. My father looks a little unsure as he steadies his foot on the stirrup. Perhaps his riding prowess has deserted him. I see Paulina standing close to a young man in gold, who, from the radiant look on her face, I guess must be Nicolo. Servants wind their way through the clusters of guests, filling glasses, offering titbits and napkins. The hunters' hounds watch their progress, slavering and whining hopefully.

I wish I had thanked him more for the present. How spoilt and how haughty I must have sounded.

Someone puts their hands over my eyes, and my heart skips. I turn around.

'Oh! It's you, Carina. H-how are you?'

'What a welcome!' she says, smiling.

'I'm sorry, I thought . . .'

'You thought I was that painter-boy,' she says, with a thin smile. 'I saw you having quite a chat with each other.'

She must have been watching through a window. 'Don't be silly,' I reply, feeling my face getting hot again.

'Aha, I see it now!' she says, pointing at me. 'It doesn't take much to get the truth out of you!' She sounds like she's only joking but tiny hairs of alarm bristle along the back of my neck. Her smile has gone, and she draws me closer, her hand on my elbow.

'You should be more careful. It's terribly easy to get a bad name, you know, and very difficult to regain a good one when you've lost it.'

I try to smile. 'Really, Carina, you're assuming something that's not the case. We were just passing inconsequential remarks. There was nothing in it.'

'I see,' she replies but her voice is granite hard – and I know that she's not convinced by my protestations at all.

24

A horn sounds, high and shrill. There are tramples and shouts and a haze of dust rises. The rest of the hunters clamber up. Raffaello leads the group to the gates and down the tree-framed track. All the others follow, trampling away in a cloud of frantic hollers and whoops.

Silence reigns after the pounding of hooves. It takes a few minutes before a new, softer set of conversations begin. Inside the lodge is sparsely furnished, and the women bustle around the table and instruct the servants in laying out the cold platters and plates. The women are smiling and busy and chatting. Some take off their shoes and elaborate hairpieces and gasp with a temporary relief.

As the hours pass, there's talk of childbirth, illnesses of older relatives, marriages and romances, the threads and turning points of human connection. Although I've little to add, the conversation is comforting, familiar. Now, among all these courtly women, I realize that I miss Giacomo. What if he should be injured by a charging horse, unseen by its rider? Will he return for the evening, or will he go back to the mainland?

I'm happy to be apart from the others, and I find a quiet

bower beside the kitchen doors, away from the bustle. Some of the other women toss a ball between them like children. Beatrice and I used to play like that, and I can almost hear her happy shrieks.

I'm called back inside to help lay the feast along with the servants. We're playing as if involved in some rustic idyll, pretending to be country wives. The real servants hardly know how to behave with this inversion of the natural order. For them, it's not a game, but a nuisance. Carina rushes in: 'They will return soon.'

It's the signal for us to be ready. Those who have taken off shoes and hairpieces put them on again. Maids brush some of the other women's hair and powder their faces.

We hear the baying hounds first, and assemble in the courtyard. Late afternoon is drifting towards evening, and the sun has dipped behind the trees. The men are sweating, shouting, calling for wine. My father looks flushed, and a little tired as he lowers himself from his steed. Another man has broken his arm in a fall, but carries the injury lightly in a sling. There's no sign of Giacomo, and from a groom I learn that a boat has already left for the island once more. The attendants parade the kill: two deer, savaged at their throats, their eyes already turning translucent. The butchery happens right there in the courtyard, and scraps are tossed to the yapping hounds, as the men regale us with the triumphs and disasters of the day.

The lodge is half open to the elements and the great table becomes gaudier and more bountiful as each dish is brought from the kitchens into the fading light. There are delicate yellow discs of polenta arranged in a curved pyramid and speckled with fresh green herbs and black pepper. Vast platters of lobsters, shrimps, mussels, octopus and clams are carried out proudly. The main focus, though, are the deer. The poor creatures slain today have been taken away, and one which has been hanging for some days is set to roast over an open fire-pit. The men are still changing from their hunting gear.

Carina comes over. She holds a fat grape, and bites into it. A little dribble of juice escapes and trickles down the side of her mouth for a second before she wipes it away.

'I'm sorry about the way I spoke to you earlier,' she says. 'I was only worried for you.'

'I know,' I say. 'Thank you.'

'I'm so glad you were able to come,' she continues. 'This must be your first hunt!'

'It's all so lovely,' I say, relieved to talk about something different.

'Yes, it is, isn't it?' she agrees. 'It's very important for everything to be perfect. This is my first time organizing the hunt as Raffaello's wife. The whole of Venice will know what we ate, and who said what, and what everyone was wearing. So tell me,' she says, and I'm afraid she's going to interrogate me about Giacomo again. 'Now that you're free, and a lady of leisure, what are your plans? Your head must still be reeling from Vincenzo's exile.'

'Every morning I wake and I feel the weight of that burden lifted,' I say. 'Though of course, I don't revel in anyone's misfortune, not even old Vincenzo's.'

Carina's face stiffens again. She leans a fraction closer,

rearranging a vase of flowers minutely, then tilting her head to survey her efforts.

'I don't imagine fortune had anything to do with it.'

She tosses out these words as though she's trying to sound light-hearted and casual, but when I look at her eyes, I see she's anything but. I wish I could steer Carina back to the mood that she's usually in. The way she's acting now – it makes me tense.

'I'm not sure I know what you mean.' I say quietly.

'Don't you?' she asks.

I lift my eyes up to her again. Her brow is arched.

'Walk with me,' she says.

We leave the tables and walk into the grounds. The water of the lake is silver and completely still. Carina clutches her long pink fan and whacks it into the palm of her hand from time to time, like a soldier with a baton.

'There may be luck in other parts of the world,' she says, 'but not in Venice. When some great stroke of fortune falls across someone's path, then the first thing I always do is look to see who threw it there. What was the chain of events? To whom is that person connected? And what actions contributed to their so-called luck?'

Her shoes crush the grassy verge on which we walk, and we have to bend from time to time to avoid the low-hanging tendrils of bindweed that dangle from the orange trees above.

'Well, in my case, I'm sure it was plain old good fortune.'

'We are either puppets, or we are puppeteers,' she says. 'Always strings attached. Always someone pulling them. That's how Venice works: it's how sailboats move; it's how the curtains in the theatre are opened at the beginning and closed at the end. It's how some people become rich and how others become poor. It's how promises are made and kept,' she says with a smile, 'and broken.'

Our walk brings us by a looping path back towards the lodge. Carina takes a few moments to issue instructions to a girl drawing water from a well. Then lowers her voice and says something that makes me go cold.

'I know, Laura. I know who you've been in contact with.'

If I try to deny it, I know that I'll give myself away. My breathing quickens, and the bones of my dress dig into my waist and chest.

'I know that the Segreta have approached you,' she continues. 'Just as they came to Beatrice.'

I stop walking. She takes a few more strides ahead, pulling a strand of foxgloves out of the ground, picking each of the little bells off and dropping them on the ground. She turns around and the look she gives me feels like a stern glare.

'What do you mean?' I say to her.

'She didn't tell you? Of course, she wouldn't have. So trustworthy. So loyal. So good at keeping her promises.' She plays with the stripped foxglove stalk like it's a little whip. 'Stay away from the Segreta. Stay well away from those women. They're not what they promise they will be. They take your secrets and they do favours in return, but that is never the end of it. Think about your poor sister. Laura, I don't want to upset or frighten you. But there are things you don't understand, and it's best not to get tangled up with such people. Their webs of control are beyond your wisdom.'

She continues away from me. Her words chime so readily with my own fears about Allegreza and the others that I hurry after her and take her arm.

'Wait! How do you know Beatrice was in contact with them? What did she tell you?' I know that I'm trembling. *If Beatrice told her, she broke the oath – she broke their first rule.*

'Most people come in contact with them sooner or later.' Her tone is lighter now and she's smiling again, but there's a troubled feeling in my stomach. 'Did they make you wear one of their masks?' Her smile turns to a grimace as she looks at her wrist. 'You're hurting me.'

I look down and see my nails are digging into her flesh. I let go at once. 'Sorry, I –'

Carina's eyes dart upwards and I turn. Allegreza is standing just a few paces away, under a bower of bay laurel. How long has she been there? I shiver. Her sudden arrival feels uncanny.

'Good evening, contessa, Signorina della Scala,' she says. She wears her usual muted grey tones – this time a deep pewter dress with a silver belt hanging from her waist. She clasps our hands between her gloved palms as we greet her in turn.

A servant girl is stuffing a large bunch of long-stemmed lilies into a high vase.

'No!' Carina shouts. The girl looks up, startled and round-eyed. 'Look at the way you're squashing them. They'll be destroyed.'

Allegreza turns her head sharply to Carina, who walks over to the table, where the nervous girl stands holding her hands away from the flowers. 'I'll show you how to do it,' Carina says more gently, 'and then you'll never forget.'

Allegreza nods then drifts away.

As Carina cuts the bruised and broken stems of the lilies with a sharp table knife, I try to drive a terrible image from my head: the gold-jawed man pushing Beatrice into the canal, while in the shadows Allegreza watches on.

25

The table at which we dined had been so inviting and lush at the beginning of the night. Now it is strewn with debris from the meal. I look at my father and will him to get up. He's slumped on one elbow and drooping, but still engaged in conversation close to the top of the table. I know he'll not even dream of leaving until the important people have started to move off.

The rhythm of a whole lifetime seems to have been squashed into these few strange hours. The excited, high-pitched, horn-blowing sounds of their beginning have descended into a low, general hum.

Nicolo, the Doge's youngest son, jumps up on to the table and strides through the debris, his boots leaving smears of black mud on the linen. He stumbles and clears his throat.

'Ladies and gentlemen, may I ask for the indulgence of your attention, please?'

Apart from me, none of the diners even look at him.

He takes his dagger from his belt and throws it. It spins around in the air, and drives its tip deep into the table. It wobbles and stiffens, wedged into its place the way I think

Nicolo wanted it to. Everyone stops talking, and a few shocked gasps rise into the air.

'I will have *attention*,' he shouts.

'Get down from there!' someone yells back.

'I'm sorry, but this is important,' Nicolo slurs.

'Well, say your piece, and have done with it,' calls the dissenting voice.

Nicolo strides forward and plucks his dagger from the table. 'Paulina di Moretti and I are going to be married,' he says.

'Ahh!' say the guests in delight and Paulina lets out a little shriek. The women rise from their seats to gather round her. Nicolo leaps athletically from the table, and the men shake his hand and slap him on the shoulder or on the back. People's faces glow in the low light of the huge candles, which once stood as tall as the jugs of wine, but now are molten masses, sliding and mixing with discarded food.

'What was the knife-throwing act all about?' mutters a woman in blue under her breath.

'Oh, it's the animal in them,' replies another. 'They're always like this when they come back from the hunt.'

Suddenly I see Paulina's face, open and sweet. I catch her eye and smile, mouthing 'Congratulations' to her across the room. She blows me a kiss in return.

I see that Allegreza is looking at Paulina too. With a jolt, I realize how my friend must appear to her – young, yes, but with an engagement to the Doge's son, also powerful. Her fine forehead crinkles thoughtfully.

Allegreza's eyes flicker and I follow the direction of her

gaze. She's staring at Carina and the count. Raffaello lifts a lock of his wife's hair and strokes her cheek with his finger. It's a simple, caring gesture, and a reminder that not every relationship in Venice is guided by necessity or ambition. I feel a rush of warmth towards them both. Carina's stern words of caution about the Segreta stemmed from concern, nothing more. There was no spite or malice in them.

Raffaello leans over to kiss her on the neck. Then his eyes seem to stare far off, and he rolls forward, his face pushed against Carina's breasts.

A young man thumps the back of Raffaello's chair. 'You haven't spent enough time in bed, Raffaello . . . that's the problem!' he laughs.

'He's looking for something he's lost!' cries someone else, raising his glass in a toast to his own words. Bellows of mirth lift the room. Still the count's face is pressed against Carina's bosom.

She says, 'Raffaello, enough!'

The joke isn't funny any more. Raffaello looks like he's in a drunken slump, not an amorous embrace. Carina tries to ease him off her. He's completely still.

She shakes her husband, gently at first, then more firmly – and then frantically.

'Raffaello! What's wrong?' she whimpers. She casts a glance to the other faces at the table. 'Why won't he move?' she asks them.

Raffaello slides in a strange slow movement on to the floor, like a puppet whose strings have been severed. Chairs scrape, some of them toppling over as people rise from their places. I rush forward too. Raffaello lies on the ground, eyes horribly open, staring at nothing.

'Stand back. Please, everyone, give him air to breathe,' begs Carina, but no amount of air will make a difference now. A man puts his fingers to Raffaello's throat, and announces, with a look of bewilderment, that he's dead. I want to go to Carina and comfort her, but it's all I can do to stay upright, so deep is the terrible feeling that swirls inside me. A young man does not simply die in the arms of his wife at a party. I don't know what has happened, but I am certain Raffaello's death was not natural.

Carina kneels beside him. She looks around the room but I don't think she sees very much at all. Her blue-green eyes seem coated with a kind of glaze. She holds out her arms like a blind woman begging for alms.

There's a buzzing in my ears. People are open-mouthed, their faces twisted like gargoyles. Others are so drunk they won't remember this tomorrow or they'll wonder if it was just a hazy dream, until someone sober tells them that it's true. The decay of this night seems to have accelerated with a frightening swiftness.

I glance at the place where Allegreza was sitting, but she has vanished.

The lodge, which felt like a palace, now feels like a cage. I must do something. This is my fault. Allegreza and the Segreta, they have killed Raffaello. I'm sure of it. Raffaello, with all his power in the Grand Council – that male power, which the wild, jealous women of the Segreta had spoken of. I saw him galloping off earlier today, and then we saw him coming back, invincible and triumphant, and surely unassailable by any weakness or illness. It makes cold, terrifying sense to me. When she was trying to warn me, Carina bad-mouthed the Society right in front of Allegreza. Their faces, I see them still, masked and flickering in the firelight, talking about how much they disapproved of the rising of men's status, and the wielding of men's power, and the vanity of men's ambition.

As the body is carried from the room, I elbow my way towards Carina.

'Move back, please. The contessa needs some space.' Amazingly, the crowd obeys me. 'Carina,' I say. 'Come with me.'

She takes my hand and her fingers feel hot around mine. She looks at me, a network of tiny veins in the whites of her eyes. Her face is smeared with tears, and the more I think that I've had a part in her horrifying predicament, the tighter I clasp her hand.

'Come,' I repeat. 'Over here.'

It's like I'm leading her through a dark forest. Some of the faces leer and pry. And even though others are kind, everybody wants to glimpse the impact of the tragedy on her face. They gather up the drama as if someone has tossed gold coins out into the crowd.

My father sits at the centre of a cluster of men. Their backs are hunched like vultures, already engaged in some debate about what all this means for the redistribution of power.

I take my friend into a room where only a single candle burns, and sit her on the couch. Carina, normally so self-assured, starts to sob.

'It must have been his heart. Are the doctors here? I must see him again. Take me back to him.'

She tries to pull away, but I hold her firmly. For a second, I see myself holding the Doge that day in the convent. Carina's mouth opens in a similar kind of twisted, tearless grimace, and she puts her hands in the air, curling her pretty fingers into rigid bent claws. I persuade her that she doesn't really want to go back. I manage to coax her to lie down, and I loosen the bodice of her dress.

I can sense someone standing silently beside me. 'Do you have a fan?' I ask.

The figure hands one to me. It's black with gold roses etched upon it.

I leap to my feet and curtsy. 'Oh, Duchess, I'm sorry!'

'Go on with what you're doing,' she says, holding up her hand. 'Please don't apologize; there's no need.'

So I take the fan and I start to wave it slowly in front of Carina.

'Perhaps she might have something to drink?' the Duchess whispers.

I search my memory of the infirmary at the convent, picturing the bottles and jars on the shelves.

'What about grappa?' I suggest. 'I've heard that's the thing for shock.'

'Quite so,' replies the Duchess, and she goes to the door to beckon someone.

When she comes back, she's holding a key in one hand and a small cup in the other. Together we sit Carina up. After she's taken a sip, we pick up a blanket that's covering a chair and together we lay it over her.

'I've told the guests to disperse,' the Duchess reassures me.

I stroke poor Carina's head. Her face is passive now, expressionless but for the eyes devoid of hope. There's nothing I can say that won't sound hackneyed. I can't pretend the loss of my sister compares to this – I've never known the love a wife has for her husband. But as the rush of my blood slows, my mind turns to darker thoughts. I remember Allegreza's standing still as a garden statue in the bower, watching us with hooded eyes. I remember Carina's warning about 'those women'. Gradually the threads are coming together, and I'm more afraid than ever to look at the tapestry they form. My breath quickens once more.

'Are *you* all right?' asks the Duchess.

She's Allegreza's cousin. Even if I could give a coherent account of my suspicions, telling her might be pointless. At worst, foolish. The Segreta's tentacles reach everywhere.

'It's just the shock,' I lie.

Soon, Carina's eyes close and, miraculously, I think she's asleep, her burst of grief spent like a sudden summer shower. Then the Duchess and I speak together in whispers. I tell her I'm not long out of the convent, but of course she already knows.

'You know the Abbess is a friend of mine.' She leans closer to me and lowers her voice, even though there's no one else present except Carina.

I glance away. 'It's probably best not to ask the Abbess about me. I wasn't exactly her favourite.'

The Duchess laughs. 'Oh, I don't take much notice of what the Abbess says. Anyway – to be perfectly honest, friends as we are, I always thought she was a wizened, sexless old crone.

Shrivelled up like a raisin. I think you were meant for a bigger world than the one she presides over.'

I talk with her as though we're old friends. I've almost forgotten I'm speaking to the wife of the Doge. For a little while, at least, the Segreta's hold doesn't feel as tight, and for once my father will be delighted.

26

Faustina's not so pleased with another new friendship I've made – a nocturnal neighbourhood tomcat, whom I've christened Nero, on account of his imperious bearing. She's forever shooing him out of the kitchen. But he's sleek and comforting and creeps up on me to nestle into my dress with disarming, arrogant familiarity. I sit in my room with the cat curled on my lap and thoughts of recent days in my mind.

Raffaello's funeral has been and gone. The word went out that the ceremony was closed to all but close family. The events of that night flash into my head, however much I wish they wouldn't. The strange blank look that fell over Raffaello's face. The smells and noises of the aftermath of the hunt, and the soft composure of the Duchess and the surprise of our easy conversation. We talked the way sisters might talk to each other, or perhaps a mother and a daughter. I stroke Nero's back. Just then, there's a heavy thud on the door.

'Come in, Father,' I sigh.

'How did you know it was me?' he asks, looming into my room.

'I have a sixth sense,' I say.

His face is grim, and he looks on the verge of anger. 'I have some *news* for you,' he says. I tense, and Nero lifts his head sleepily.

'What is it?'

He plucks a scroll from inside his jacket. 'A letter,' he says. 'About you.'

Several possibilities present themselves, but the most frightening is that I haven't been careful enough regarding the Segreta. Perhaps someone has found out about my midnight assignations. The consequences don't bear thinking of.

'Oh yes?' I manage.

Suddenly, his face breaks into a grin. 'My dear,' he says with an exaggerated flourish. 'It's from the wife of the Doge. The Duchess herself. Can you credit it?'

He tosses the scroll on the bed. The cat jumps off my lap and scurries away.

Dear Antonio,
You would do me the greatest honour if you would permit a likeness
of your daughter to be hung in the Ducal residence. Since the tragic
events at Count Raffaello's residence, I've thought upon her many
times, and in recognition of her kindness that night, I would like to
commission a portrait by an artist of my choosing. I trust this will be
acceptable.
Yours ever,
Besina

'Do you understand what this means?' My father dances around the room like he's a little child. 'She'll send a ducal artist. They'll paint you in a perfect light and put your portrait in the palace corridor! The Continent's rulers and their sons will see your face and ask about you! In no time we'll have found a match for you and, my darling girl, don't you see? The family will be saved.'

I cannot quite find the right words. 'I thought the Doge didn't care for the della Scalas any longer,' I say. 'You said we should have two, three minutes at least.'

My father grins and wags a finger at me. 'Don't get clever with me, my girl,' he says. He claps his hands and leaves the room, muttering, 'All will be well!'

His certainty weighs heavily on me, but somehow it also manages to make me feel happy and a little powerful. What strange mixtures of things I've felt since I stepped out of the doors of the convent. What concoctions of fear and excitement and despair and joy. I wish I could disentangle all of them and feel just one thing at a time, but it doesn't seem possible any more.

For two nights I sleep with lavender and thyme leaves under my pillow, and that aromatic combination lingers in my dreams. I see a picture of myself hanging on the corridors of the Doge's palace. The same picture falls into dark waters, and looms behind the head of the Abbess as she caresses the bookmark ribbon of her Bible the way she always used to do. And in my dream the picture changes. First I'm in my brown novice's clothes, then the resplendent liquid red dress that so dazzled me when I first wore it. Finally that becomes the heavy wet clothes that my sister wore the night she drowned. On my face is the swan-feather mask.

I wake sweating. Beatrice knew the Segreta too. She trusted them, so Carina says, and look what fate befell her. I wonder just how embroiled she became.

I'm to sit for my portrait in the morning. Faustina bustles into my room and tells me that Bianca is making a special breakfast, 'to get your colour up'. The portrait will be completed here, in the back salon, where the light will be at its best.

After I've bathed, Faustina brings one of my mother's dresses down to me. 'Your father requested that you wear this,' she says. She disappears again, and leaves me with the garment. The finest shell pink silk with shimmers of pearl. White velvet lattice on the bodice, and tendrils of darker pink hanging at the waist. I think I remember her wearing it. Echoes of its colour and its tone are mixing in my mind with the sound of my mother's singing.

'I've set the painter up in the salon,' Bianca says, peering around the door. She's blushing slightly, which I think is rather strange for a girl as bold as she is.

Faustina smoothes my hair, smiling with pride. 'Come now, Laura. I'm to attend the sitting.'

She speaks as if it's an invitation to a royal wedding. I'm touched by her excitement, but can't imagine it'll be that interesting an event. At least Faustina's presence will mean I won't die of boredom, sitting still for hours.

Faustina leads me down the stairs, carefully holding the hem of my dress clear of the floor as I walk. She pushes open the salon door and ushers me inside.

The painter stands at the far end of the room with his back

to us — and I know. I know by the curve of his back and the way his feet are planted on the ground, and the way his hands are resting on his hips. I don't even have to see his face.

It's him.

And suddenly I hope Bianca and Faustina really have made me as beautiful as I could ever possibly look.

27

Giacomo turns around, and his eyebrows disappear for a second under the curls of his fringe; he knocks a jar of water on the floor, but doesn't even seem to notice.

'That's not the greatest start to proceedings, is it?' Faustina tuts. 'We expected a painter, not a vandal.' But I can see her eyes twinkle as she hurries towards the broken glass, clearly charmed by this handsome man.

'Please don't exert yourself on behalf of my clumsiness,' says Giacomo. 'I'll clear everything up.'

Again he's dressed in that loose white shirt. A silver pendant hangs around his neck, and his skin is olive beneath, and perfectly smooth like polished wood. He holds my gaze and smiles, and I hope Faustina doesn't see me flush.

'I'll just sit in the corner here,' she says. 'Don't take any notice of me.'

She carries her basket of embroidery over to the chair and gets to work. Loudly she settles herself, humming a little tune. Amazing how my kind old nursemaid could have been transformed so quickly into this noisy intruder! All I want to do is talk to him.

'Greetings, Signorina della Scala,' says Giacomo.

It should have been an ordinary thing for me to hear someone say my name, but I'm enchanted by the sound of it coming from his mouth.

'Would you like to take a seat?' he says, gesturing to a chair positioned by the window. I do so, and he strides over, circling behind me.

'Would you mind?' he says, lightly touching my shoulders and turning them a fraction.

As he makes his way back to his easel, my father sweeps in.

'Ah, yes, excellent,' he says, clapping his hands together. 'Boy, can I speak with you for a moment?'

Carefully Giacomo sets down his stick of charcoal and my father takes him aside. There's some muttering, and then he hands Giacomo a few coins.

'Signor, it isn't necessary,' says Giacomo. 'The commission has been paid for.'

'Please,' says my father. 'I want your best work. You'll receive the same again if you deliver it.'

Giacomo blushes and places the coins in his pocket. After my father has gone, Giacomo moves his easel closer, so that we're only a few paces apart. Giacomo, his eyes flicking from me to the canvas, goes to work. I'm not sure where I'm supposed to look, so I lower my eyes.

'Look up, please,' he says, with professional seriousness. 'I can't paint your eyes unless I can see them.'

I stare at him, smiling.

'And no smiling,' he adds, though one tugs at the corners of his lips.

I smile more, then gather myself. I wonder if I'm allowed to speak. Probably not. The silence, but for the scraping of his outlines, is hypnotic. He's not the only one who is painting a picture. Even though it looks like I'm just sitting there with my face tilted to the sun, I too am capturing his likeness. I relish this opportunity to look on him without embarrassment. His nose, I see, is delicate and slightly upturned, his jaw, shaded a little with an even beard. He chews his lower lip and the creases by his eyes deepen as he concentrates.

The silence is broken by a rasping snuffle. It's Faustina, snoring softly in the big-cushioned chair, her sewing dropped idly in her lap.

His face softens. 'How are you, Laura?' he whispers and from his lips, my Christian name sounds almost dangerous. 'I was worried, especially after the awful news about the count. Your friend must be very shaken.'

'It was a terrible night,' I say.

He takes a little pot of paint and a tiny trowel and he pastes some of it on to the palette he holds in his hand.

'Is that your secret blue?' I ask him.

'No,' he says, 'I'm trying to mix something completely new, another colour that no one has been able to make before. But I fear, my lady, that I'll fail.'

'Why?'

'Because I'm trying to find a way of capturing your eyes, and I'm in despair.'

A shudder passes through me, like pleasure and panic mixed together. From another, the easy charm would make me roll my eyes, but his troubled look disarms me, and I laugh. He walks past the easel, coming towards me. He puts out his hand and holds my chin and he tilts my face up a little. I close my eyes. I keep them closed for a couple of seconds.

'There,' he says, 'that should do it.'

When I open them again, he's walking back to the easel, saying, 'You know, if we spend the whole day in silence, the hours will pass very slowly.'

Faustina snorts and shifts in her sleep.

'I wasn't sure if I was allowed to speak.'

He picks up his palette. 'Some artists are like that, but not me,' he says. 'I like to know about the person I'm painting.'

'Did you finish your sketches of the hunt?' I ask.

'Some,' he said. 'But they're only preparatory drawings. I heard that you took care of your friend.'

How would he know this? I suppose that servants talk and gossip as much as their masters, if not more.

'It seems so strange that poor Raffaello would have been so full of life one moment, and then the next . . . just gone,' I say.

'It seems in Venice that death is never natural. At least not the cases that I've heard about.'

'You don't think it was natural?' I ask. 'They say his heart was in poor condition.'

Giacomo shakes his head. 'It didn't seem so to me.'

His certainty, tallying as it does with my worst suspicions, makes me a little angry. How could a painter know what happened?

'You seem very sure of your opinions,' I say, more harshly than I intend. He doesn't seem to notice.

'Everyone in Venetian society is part of a scheme or a plot.

If you're lucky, you can disentangle yourself from it – but if you're not, then you go the way of Raffaello.'

His blunt dismissal of Carina's husband doesn't quell my rising temper. Faustina would probably be delighted with the colour in my cheeks if she were awake and could see them now.

'You think it was *his* fault he was killed?'

Giacomo looks at me with concern. 'Probably not,' he says. 'Chin up, please.'

I think he's only saying this to steer the conversation back to safer waters, but my mind has returned to my sister. *She* wasn't part of any scheme, I'm sure of that. Not my sweet, innocent Beatrice.

'I've upset you,' he says. 'I've spoken out of turn. Accept my apologies.'

'Nonsense,' I reply. 'Please, tell me more about the life of a painter.'

'It would bore you, I think.'

'It must be more interesting than the life of an unmarried woman,' I reply.

'I expect, then, that your life won't be dull for much longer. You'll have suitors queuing all the way to the harbour.'

'Is your skill with a brush so great?'

His eyes seem warm as he looks at me. 'It doesn't need to be,' he says.

Faustina sits up suddenly. 'Yes, yes, Antonio . . .' she says confusedly. As she comes to her senses, her eyes focus on us. 'That's good. Back to work.' Her eyes droop shut and her plump chest rises and falls.

'Where do you live?' I ask Giacomo.

'Sometimes at the Duke's palace,' he says, 'with one of the grooms. But I rent a small studio down by the Lido. Mathieu takes care of it. It can be noisy, but the people there are like family to me. I'm sure you'd like them too.'

'It sounds wonderful,' I tell him. 'What are your friends like? What do they do?'

'They're actors, painters, poets. I know a couple of mathematicians too, but they're not quite as much fun as everyone else.'

'I'm sure they're more exciting than merchants,' I say. 'All that Father's friends seem to care about are trading routes and fair winds.'

He laughs as he mixes more paints and takes a brush from a jar of water.

'I love the sound of your Venice,' I say to him. 'All I've seen of the city has been about money and power and the comforts of the body – never, as far as I can make out, anything to do with beauty or the soul.'

'If it's my Venice, then it can be your Venice too.'

For a wonderful, soaring moment, I think he may be right.

'And how do you know the Doge?' I ask. 'It's quite a responsibility to paint the ceilings of the most powerful man in Venice.'

'It is indeed,' he says, not looking up from his canvas. 'As for how I know him, I forged a letter of recommendation.'

I'm shocked. 'You did what?'

'I'm joking,' he said. 'Actually, I've just had another large commission that I've been bursting to tell someone about. The Doge wants me to do a fresco inside St Mark's.'

'The *cathedral*?'

'I know. It feels like a very great responsibility.'

'I think St Mark's is the most beautiful building in all of Venice.'

He smiles. 'I do too,' he says. 'The commission is for the chapel where his son is buried.'

I start, remembering the two tombs lying silently together. I'm relieved that he's focused on his palette, daubing a yellow pigment on to it.

A little shadow of concern seems to flicker across his face. 'I'm not supposed to tell anyone. It's a big secret.'

'Aha!' I laugh. 'So you have a secret too, then, like everyone in Venice!'

He doesn't laugh. He doesn't even smile.

'You can trust me,' I say. But a shiver ripples up to the surface of my skin, because I've just remembered the last time I said those words.

He works in silence while I hunt around for something to say that will restore the easy feeling between us. I'm relieved when he finally shakes his head at me, pretending to scold.

'Stop moving about so much,' he says with a grin. 'I can't paint you unless you're still.'

'Sorry,' I say.

And this whole time I feel the quickening thump of my heart as if it's trying to escape from my body. I hope he doesn't notice. It would be a hard thing to explain.

I've no idea how much time has passed. But the sun has moved across the window, and it must be getting late. Faustina wakes up with a snort. She sits upright like a puppet whose strings have been pulled, looking dazed.

'How long have I been asleep?' she asks dozily, and I tell her it's probably been hours. She's horrified and tells me off for not waking her, then scuttles away to find Bianca.

Giacomo starts to gather his materials. He cleans the brush and wraps it in a greying cloth. He fastens the lids on the pots of paint he's been using, then loads them into his basket.

'Is it finished?' I ask him.

'You're a demanding client,' he laughs. 'I couldn't capture that face in a single sitting.'

'That means you'll have to come back again.'

'Yes, it does,' he says. 'Do you mind?'

I shake my head. I wouldn't mind if he came back a hundred times, and a hundred times after that. I'm trying not to smile, but there seems to be no controlling this wayward face of mine.

'May I see it?' I ask.

'Not until it's finished. It's bad luck.'

'I'm not superstitious,' I say. 'Please?'

He wipes his hands on a stained cloth. 'If you want to look, then I don't imagine I, or anybody else, would be able to stop you. Now, I'd better go and clean up.' He excuses himself and leaves the room, closing the door behind him.

I stand stiffly. The other side of the canvas draws me like a powerful hand, so much that I can't resist. I gather myself and then I walk around.

Pink and pale, I'm transparent, like a ghost or a shadow passing a window. But already the portrait has taken shape, and an image is starting to emerge. In Giacomo's picture I'm strong and upright.

On the low table beside the easel is a big black leather satchel with the flap open. Visible inside it are stacks of papers and the lines of other drawings. Something draws me to it and makes me want to look, even though it's an intrusion. Carefully, I pull out a handful and leaf through. Talent resides in every one of them. The perfectly executed arches of churches, the curves of fruit and pottery, the shapes of faces, bodies, arms and legs.

Three sheaves slide out, floating down on to the floor. I crouch quickly, my mother's shell-pink dress rising around me as I rush to recover them. I turn over the first. It's a sketch of a woman's body – just a detail from her chin to her waist. She's lying on a couch with one arm above her head. She wears a peasant's dress, and something about the picture feels very intimate. Who is this girl to him? Who is he to her? The modesty that I learned in the convent makes me blush, though no one is here to see my shame.

The second picture shows the same model, though in this she leans over a desk, holding a quill as she writes a letter. Her long brown hair falls over her face, but there's something familiar about her pose. It reminds me of myself in the convent, when I used to write my letters to Beatrice.

I hear Giacomo's footsteps, soft scuffs against the marble. He's whistling happily as he approaches. Panic shoots through me. What will he think when he sees me crouched on the floor, going through his pictures? I should never have looked! I scoop up the sheaves of parchment, but as I pack them back into the satchel, Giacomo enters the room. His painting tools and brushes are all wrapped up in a bundle of white cloth and there is a secret smile on his face. I can't stop myself from trembling. The words of apology are already forming on my lips when the third picture slides from my grasp and floats to the floor. It shows the same girl – but this time her face looks defiantly into my own.

A constricted little wail escapes my lips.

'What's the matter?' asks Giacomo. His smile vanishes.

I hold out the picture to him with a trembling hand. I want it taken from me. But I can't let it go.

It's a picture of Beatrice.

28

I slowly put the picture on the table between us and step back. I cling on to the sides of my dress, crushing the material between my fists. 'How is it that you have drawings of my sister in your portfolio?'

'I can explain —'

'Her bodice is unfastened!'

The truth stabs through me. I'm sure it was him — that Giacomo was the man my sister went to see the night she died. The pictures, so full of sensuality and longing, leave me little doubt. Giacomo and Beatrice were lovers.

I take a couple more backwards steps, moving closer to the door.

'Laura, I'm sorry I didn't tell you.'

'Tell me what?' I say. My voice sounds high and loud.

'That I knew your sister.'

'What possible reason was there not to tell me something as important as that?' My teeth are clamped together. 'Why would you keep it a secret? Why would anyone? Unless they had something to hide.'

'It wasn't like that.'

'Like what?'

He looks nervously at the door. Has he just been playing with me – the lingering looks and the lovely things he's said?

'Laura, please . . .'

'Oh yes, of course. Little Laura, fresh from the convent, naive about everything. That's what people think. Well, I'm not stupid. I know that my father was right. There are no friends in Venice.'

'Don't say that. It's not true.' He walks closer to me and tries to take my hand.

I snatch my fingers away and run out of the room, across the hall, through the front gates. I keep running along the banks of the slick black canal. The wind strengthens and it's starting to rain. The drops on my skin are like tiny knives.

I travel all the way to St Mark's on foot, crossing the Rialto and other tiny bridges, and threading narrow alleys. I rush inside. I don't know why I've been drawn here. I kneel at the back of the pews and put my face in my hands. Rainwater drips from the ends of my hair, and a little pool of it collects on the floor. Jesus's broken body, betrayed and bleeding, hangs before me.

God, please show me someone I can trust.

I'm ashamed when I remember how far I thought I had come – what a sophisticated lady of the city I thought I had grown into.

There's a poor man hunched a couple of rows ahead of me, clacking his rosary beads. A woman lights candles in Our Lady's chapel. Two shadowy people flit around, stopping at the Stations of the Cross. Nobody comes near me. I'm like La

Lunatica from the convent who used to rock to and fro, alone in her cell.

I remain on my knees, offering rambling prayers, until my skin seems to register my cold damp clothes at last, and I shiver. I don't know if God will answer any of my entreaties, but being here in the dark soothes me. I breathe deeply and realize that perhaps I've found a serenity of sorts.

I stand, holding on to the railing of the pew in front of me. I wipe my face with a handkerchief that I've found in the pocket of my mother's dress. I breathe it in, hoping for a lingering smell of her, but there are no vestiges of Gabriela della Scala in that little square of cloth.

Just as I'm ready to go back out into the world, the door of the cathedral creaks open, and a black-hooded woman enters. She stands upright, with her head up high, and carries a bouquet of flowers in her arms as tenderly as if it was a baby. She genuflects towards the altar then walks up to the tombs of Carlo and Roberto. It seems like a lifetime since Paulina and I stood in front of them, considering the story of the feuding families and their terrible end. The woman kneels down in front of Carlo's tomb, pulls her hood off her head to reveal flashes of silver hair.

It's Grazia – Carlo and Carina's mother.

There's something mesmerizing about the way she polishes the gilded edges of her son's tomb, and arranges the great armful of roses at its base. She kneels, her hands clasped and her head bowed. It's wrong to be watching her grief like this. I should leave.

But the door has swung open again. A woman hurries in,

shaking raindrops from her long yellow cape. Anger rises in my chest — it's the prostitute who wore my sister's ring. Her brown eyes flicker around the cathedral, then rest on Grazia. She moves towards her.

I follow, staying behind the pillars so I'm hidden from view. I wonder if Grazia is in danger. The prostitute glides down and kneels beside Carina's mother, so close to her that their shoulders are almost touching.

Grazia turns to the other woman, and from her slow movements, it's clear that she's not alarmed. She takes the woman's shoulders and kisses her on both cheeks. They know each other. But what is this woman of ill repute to Grazia de Ferrara? Carina's mother reaches into her black cloak and pulls out a stringed purse. The prostitute takes it with the hand that still wears my sister's ring; I see it glitter in the candlelight.

My thoughts approach a dark threshold of understanding, God has led me to the truth, so all I have to do is to reach out and grab it. Grazia is a member of the Segreta; this woman has Beatrice's ring. I know now that I am looking at Beatrice's murderer. Or one of them at least. What better intermediary to use, in hiring a killer, than a woman of the streets? Is she only now paying off this woman for the deadly services, or is this fee for some other vicious act she's delivered on behalf of the Sisterhood?

Without offering prayers of her own, the prostitute stands and quickly leaves the cathedral through a side door. I hurry after her.

The rain has stopped, but there are still huge sheets of water on the ground. Merchants, beggars and nobles go about their business, some glancing in my direction as I run. I catch up with the woman when she's almost in the very centre of St Mark's Square, and I grab her shoulder and spin her around. I remember her struggles last time and hold her firmly by the arms.

She shrugs and wriggles to disentangle herself from me. 'You,' she says. 'Take your hands off me!'

'Who are you?' I ask. 'What did you do to my sister?'

She tries to pull free her arm, but I twist her wrist with a strength I didn't know I had. She gasps. 'I'm Bella Donna, and I know nothing of your sister, I swear.'

'Then tell me how you're wearing her ring!' I hiss, holding her hand up between us.

A wave of sunlight has broken through drifting clouds over the square and the vast puddles glint on the ground. Thin blankets of steam rise around the square. An old man watches us beneath a dripping porch.

'How dare you!' screeches the woman.

'Tell me!'

She stops fighting, but fire burns in her eyes. 'This ring was a gift. Now will you let me go?'

Her tone is so straightforward that I loosen my grip. She scurries off between two covered stalls. I run into the lane after her, splashing through puddles and across a wooden bridge. Her feet slap the ground as she barges past two mystified gentlewomen, who frown and tut as she passes. 'Watch where you're going!' one says to her, but I doubt she hears.

I can't keep up. When I round the next corner, the alley splits into three. I follow one with hurried steps, but it's clear that either I've chosen the wrong turn, or she's quicker than the wind.

At last I know who's behind Beatrice's death – and I've lost her.

29

As I walk home, I stumble on a tiny piazza that I've never seen before. It's empty. The shutters of the buildings that loom on each side are closed and an unexpected silence helps me to calm my beating heart. I sit in the middle, on a bench of stone, and try to stop the world from swimming in front of me. Small streets lead away in many directions. Shadows fall. Footsteps echo. I watch the raindrops cling to my mother's sodden dress.

I'm sick at heart. The Segreta tried to make me feel grateful and obliged for banishing Vincenzo. Raffaello is dead because of the powers that are controlling me – the same powers, I'm sure, that killed my sister. I'm glad that I haven't followed Allegreza's orders and recruited someone for the Society now. I refuse to lure some poor trusting soul the same way I've been ensnared.

I'm sick too of being dressed up and primped and powdered, to lure some rich man who'll solve my father's financial woes. And, to add to all of this, Giacomo's betrayal . . . How could he keep such a secret from me? Even when I held the proof in my hands, still he showed no shame.

His words had seemed like magic things to me. I could

nearly taste them, like sips of wine. But they were lies, masquerading in the honeyed lilt of the boy I thought I might be falling for.

Oh, Beatrice, I think. *Did he treat you like this too?*

Annalena once said that we have more power than we know, inside our own hearts. I wonder if she's right. I need such power now.

It's nearly dark when I get home. Giacomo and the half-finished canvas have gone. I'll be happy never to set eyes on him again. I dash up into my room, leaving a damp snail's trail across the marble floor, and peel off my sodden clothes. I rub my hair dry and dab myself with perfume to disguise the musky smell of Venetian rain that seems to seep from every pore.

Faustina is at the door. 'Thanks be to God,' she says. 'Laura, you promised you wouldn't disappear like this! I was sure we would have to search the streets for you. The painter almost convinced me to start, but . . .' She wrings her hands. 'Oh, Laura, where did you go? And your dress!'

'I just needed to be on my own, that's all.'

She takes my hands. 'Darling, you're freezing.' She takes a woollen shawl and puts it round my shoulders. 'Carina sent a message,' she adds. 'She asked if she might call here tomorrow afternoon. I told her of course.'

I plead a cold to avoid dinner with my father. There's much I have to tell him, about Beatrice and Allegreza, but I need to steel myself for the conversation first. I only hope I can make him understand what the women of the Segreta are capable of. Each time I think of my confession, I hear Allegreza's low tones. *Breathe one word of the Segreta to anyone – and your life will be forfeit*. Each time I close my eyes, I see the masks crowding around.

Sleep comes more easily than I expect and I doze well into the morning. My head is clear. I'll talk with my father now. He won't be able to ignore what I tell him of Beatrice's final hours. And if I stay within these walls, no one, not even the Segreta, can touch me.

Faustina hears me stirring and comes to help me dress.

'I wish I could sleep as you do,' she says, tugging my green gown over my shoulders. 'But alas, I barely manage a fitful slumber.'

I remember her snores while Giacomo was painting, and would smile if it weren't for the memory of what had followed.

I ask her my father's whereabouts and she says he's in his library.

'Come with me,' I say. 'We need to talk to him.'

'What do you mean, child?' she asks, trailing in my wake.

I don't answer; she could barely bring herself to describe Beatrice's death to me, and I don't want her to run away. If she's present when I lay out the story before my father, I can appeal for her corroboration. I try to formulate my words. *Father, Beatrice was murdered*. Or, *Father, I must tell you a dreadful thing. Sit down*.

I knock and my father calls me inside. He's already sitting in the ancient leather chair where my mother used to read me stories. Faustina wrings her hands beside me, as though she's sensed that some extra duty will shortly befall her.

'Father –' I begin.

A cough by the window catches me. A woman stands there, her silver-streaked hair reflecting the morning light.

Allegreza.

'Ah, here she is,' chuckles my father. 'Just the person we wanted to talk to.'

I bow my head a little and make a cautious curtsy in Allegreza's direction. What's she doing here? Has she heard already about my pursuit of Bella Donna through the rain-soaked square?

'How nice to see you, Allegreza,' I say politely, though I wonder if she hears the wariness in my voice.

'Likewise,' smiles Allegreza. 'There is a recital this afternoon, in honour of Nicolo and Paulina's impending marriage. I was just asking your father if you'd like to accompany me to it. I have seen that you and Paulina are close friends.'

My father darts me one of his expectant glances. I think quickly.

'You're very kind to think of me, but I'm afraid I'm expecting a visitor this afternoon – Carina. I haven't seen her since her husband's death. I don't want to be out when she calls.'

My father sits up in his chair. 'Nonsense, Laura. This recital starts in an hour. You'll be back in plenty of time.' He turns to Allegreza. 'Won't she?'

'It's up to her whether she wants to come or not. I wouldn't like to *compel* anyone,' Allegreza replies. The line of her jaw tightens.

'Well,' my father speaks with a heavy, deliberate tone. 'I know that my daughter shares my view that attending such a wonderful event would be a privilege. Isn't that right, Laura?'

I see Faustina shoot me a troubled glance; she senses my reluctance. But the combined force is too much. *Calma*, I tell myself. Bide your time. Don't give yourself away. 'Yes, of course, Father. How silly of me. I would be pleased to join you, Signora di Rocco.'

I thought the sun was going to come out, but when we leave my father's house great swathes of cloud lurk in the sky. Allegreza holds out her arm and reluctantly I slip my hand inside it.

'Where is the recital taking place?' I ask.

'Wait and see.'

We walk together in silence, snaking through the city along corridors of stone. I wish I had requested that Faustina or Bianca join us, but I expect Allegreza would've had a clever answer to that too. At each corner, my skin prickles with fear as I imagine Bella Donna leaping towards me. I try to think rationally. Surely Allegreza would not have come to collect me in person from my father if she intended that I never return?

We turn down a grubby alley and reach a cracked and stained wooden doorway. Allegreza takes out a key and turns it in the lock.

'There isn't a recital for Paulina and Nicolo, is there?' I say.

'Not quite,' she smiles.

'Then where are you taking me?' I start to back away.

'Please don't be alarmed,' she says, catching my arm. 'I'm sorry for the deceit. It was to keep your father from suspecting anything.'

She opens the door and ushers me in, then closes it behind

us and locks it again. At our feet, steep stone steps lead down. Allegreza has to stoop to avoid the low ceiling. Moss and strange little white stalactites hang from above, as if we are in a cave, and the smell of damp hangs in the air. I pause at the base of the stairs.

'Come, come. You're one of us, Laura. There's no need to be afraid.'

A few candles cast a dim glow ahead, and the space opens out into a large cellar lined with old racks and bottles. Six or seven of the Segreta wait in their expressionless masks. I haven't brought mine, and for a moment I feel so exposed I might as well be naked. I recognize Grazia in her black cat mask. *I know* your *secret*, I think, fighting back the temptation to denounce her then and there; to tell her that I saw her in the cathedral yesterday. But the door is locked behind me. Reveal her secret now and it would blossom and die unseen. In all likelihood, I would die with it. I swallow, thickly.

'What will happen when my father finds out there has been no recital?' I whisper to Allegreza.

'He won't find out.'

'How can you be so sure?'

'Because nobody will tell him.' She says it as if it's a steadfast fact. She puts on her owl mask and her eyes fix on mine, as if daring me to challenge her.

One of the dark figures brushes my shoulder. It's the woman in the fox mask.

'Hello, Laura,' she says, and hands me a mask decorated with peacock's feathers. As soon as I put it on, I feel strangely safer.

'Welcome, sisters, to this special meeting,' announces Allegreza.

I wonder if I'm the first item on the agenda. Will there be retribution for my attack on Bella Donna? Will they want to know why I haven't secured a new member?

But then I realize that they consider me part of the crowd – no more a focus of attention than anyone else.

'I would like you all to meet someone. Maria!' Allegreza beckons with her long fingers. 'Please bring our new guest forward.'

One of the masked women opens a door to an antechamber. She leads out a girl dressed in golden satin, a black band tied about her eyes. My throat is dry.

It's Paulina.

Maria takes off the blindfold. Paulina trembles, staring around the room. 'What do you want from me?'

Paulina, fiancée to the Doge's son – a perfect recruit for the Segreta. Did they tire of waiting for me to deliver her? I wish I could tear off my mask and run to her and take her away from here. But if I stay hidden I may be better able to protect her.

Allegreza explains the rules of the Society in solemn detail, just as she did to me. Paulina nods her head. She tells everyone she has a secret, and there's that unsettling swollen silence that I've heard before.

Paulina stands firm, looking around. 'What I have to tell you is that there's another secret society. A society that Count Raffaello established.'

Some of the women bless themselves at the sound of the dead man's name.

Paulina's voice grows more confident as she continues. 'Raffaello was the founder of a gambling society. He's been gaining members throughout Venice and beyond, stirring people up to get involved. He sat at tables during which great fortunes were won and lost. Every day the stakes grow higher and higher.'

Horrified, I remember my father's argument with Raffaello that day while Carina and I sat in the courtyard. I think of my mother's missing jewels, the blank spaces where pictures used to hang.

'He was playing a very dangerous game,' she continues. 'Most people who knew what he was up to are surprised it took this long for him to meet his end.'

I knew it. Raffaello was murdered.

Paulina is ushered back into the antechamber. We huddle together to deliberate on the value of her secret while she waits.

'How much value is this to us really?' one woman says. 'The dogs on the streets know that Raffaello's death was not an accident. Everyone knows that someone killed him, poisoned him probably.'

Can she really not see the truth before her eyes – that the killers stand among us now? For the first time, I wonder if there are secrets even within the Society. Depths of shadow. Or is this all an act for my benefit? Perhaps I'm the *only* one here being kept in the dark, and behind these masks the women are laughing.

'True,' Allegreza replies, 'but the real point is the information about the gambling club. That's something that is valuable for us to know. She may be able to tell us more. Who the other members are, perhaps.'

My father, among them, I think. Despite everything, I can't bear to think of him brought to public shame.

'I propose we vote to accept her into the Society,' Allegreza concludes. 'All those in favour, say yes.'

A flurry of yeses bounce around the walls.

'All those against, say no.'

There's silence. No one would heed my lone dissenting voice, so I say nothing – La Muta.

'Our decision is made,' announces Allegreza.

We move apart. Silk and feather swish past wood and stone, and Paulina is summoned.

She stands tall and expectant in the middle of the room, and the ritual of welcome is conducted. Allegreza takes her hand and scores the palm with the tip of her knife. We watch as a line of blood appears. Paulina is serene, still, smiling. Does she have any idea what she's getting herself into?

Grazia gives her a glorious dark purple mask shaped like a blowsy flower, the eye-holes edged with turquoise stones. 'And now, Paulina, is there anything we can do for you?'

Paulina's smile becomes a little coy. 'There is a girl . . .' she begins. She speaks of the young woman we met that day by the street performers, the one who sniggered behind her fan. A daughter of the man Paulina's uncle worked for, I remember. Paulina says hesitantly that she wants this girl – Perlita is her name – to suffer an embarrassment, in public. It's a petty, malicious desire, and though the masks prevent me from seeing the reactions in the other women's faces, I'm not surprised when Allegreza shakes her head. 'Such a thing is not becoming,' she says. 'We behave according to a code of honour.'

I almost scoff and Paulina flushes. 'Well, I . . . I . . .'

'No matter,' Grazia interrupts. 'There will come a time, I'm sure, when we can help you.'

Paulina regains her composure, and the women break away to talk among themselves. I draw close to her side. 'Congratulations, Paulina.'

I can see her eyes widen behind her mask. 'Laura?' There's a sliver of dismay in her voice. 'Is that you? You never . . .'

'Shh,' I interrupt. I lean towards her, so that only she might hear my words. 'Be careful. The Society isn't what it seems.'

'But *you're* a member,' she replies. 'What do you mean?'

Allegreza is suddenly beside us, like an apparition. 'Paulina, excuse me, but I need to have a word with Laura.'

She gestures for me to come to the edge of the gathering and I do as I'm bidden.

'You seem troubled, Laura. Is something wrong?'

'Why, should there be?' I reply.

She takes off her mask, and looks at me directly, so I do the same. 'Venice is a dangerous and frightening place,' she says gently. 'We must trust one another.'

Who is she trying to fool? She must think I'm as stupid as Giacomo does. I see Paulina chattering to the women the way she does when she's at any party. They've lured my friend into their web, and they spin the gossamer around her.

'I don't believe you,' I say.

Her face flinches as though I've slapped her.

I move towards the door. 'I have to go home. Carina will be calling soon, and I don't want to let her down.'

Allegreza doesn't try to stop me. She follows me up the

stairs and unlocks the door to let me out. 'Be careful,' she says. Her voice is deep and concerned. 'Remember, Laura, how I said you are bound to us? Well, we are bound to you too. If ever you're in danger, come to me.'

I nod and walk off into the afternoon sun, but I can't imagine ever asking for their help again. When I glance back, she stands there, a tall shadow in the doorway.

30

Carina is waiting for me in the salon, a pale and thin version
of herself. Bianca is laying out a jug of lemon juice mixed with
water and sugar. She pours it into two goblets.

'Where have you been?' Carina asks.

I go to her, and take her cold hands in mine. 'I'm so sorry.
I . . .'

She's started to cry, so I fold her in my arms. 'Bianca, leave
us, please.'

I take Carina by the hand and lead her to my mother's soft
chair. I offer her a handkerchief.

'I feel so lost without him,' she says after a time, 'and if I
could find . . .' She looks at me, and there's fear within her.
'Can I trust you, Laura?'

'On my dear sister's memory,' I say.

She takes a deep breath, and glances towards the door.

'Bianca has gone,' I say.

Carina nods. 'They have spies everywhere.'

'Who?'

'You know,' she whispers.

Her look implores me to utter the word, to break my vow to Allegreza. But even now I can't.

'The Segreta!' she finishes.

I take a sip of juice. In all likelihood, Carina doesn't know of her own mother's involvement with the Society.

'I think they killed Beatrice too,' I say. It's the first time I've given voice to my suspicions, and saying the words strengthens my conviction.

Carina sits up, frowning. 'Do you have proof?'

I shake my head, and relate as well as I can the evidence I have seen with my own eyes. I omit my own involvement with the masked women but the gaps in my story are obvious, and Carina reads the empty space for what it is.

'My God!' she says. 'You're one of them, aren't you?' She begins to stand, but I beg her not to go.

'One of them in name, but not in nature,' I say. 'They tricked me, with the promise to break my engagement to Vincenzo.'

She sighs deeply. 'If what you say is true, then you – then we – must tread carefully.'

'I swear on my mother's grave, on my sister's too, that I'm not lying. There must be someone we can tell – someone on the Grand Council, perhaps.'

Her face is hard. 'No! Raffaello knew of them too, and Beatrice, and look what happened to them. We must keep this to ourselves, until we're sure.'

'I am sure,' I say.

'Until we are sure it's safe.'

I wish I could talk to Carina about Giacomo, about the gnawing sensation like hunger in my stomach. But I still feel foolish for believing his sugared words, and my hurt seems nothing while the shadows of the Segreta loom over our conversation like squatting vultures.

After she's gone, having first extracted a promise that I won't behave rashly – 'and under no circumstances talk to your father' – I kick off my shoes and throw myself on to my bed. About this time I would be heading for evening prayer in the convent. Back then my life was so ordered that every moment of each day was accounted for; now I feel like a gondolier who has left the safety of the canals, steering through twisting currents and trying not to be swept out to sea.

There's a little rap on my door. I snatch up my mother's book of love poems from under my pillows and pretend to be absorbed in its pages.

It's Bianca. She looks like she's trying not to smirk.

'That man has called again,' she says.

'What man?'

'You know, Giacomo. The painter.'

I scramble from the bed and stand on the cold floor. 'Well, you must tell the *painter* to go away this instant, and not to come here again.'

Bianca opens her mouth to interrupt, but I hold up my hand.

'You must tell him that I won't sit for him today, or any other. Make sure he gets my message. And come back and tell me when he's gone.'

'That's what I'm trying to tell you. He's already gone. He just came to deliver the painting.'

'Deliver it? It isn't finished.'

'He says it is,' says Bianca.

He can't possibly have finished it. Only yesterday it was just a ghostly outline. There were supposed to be at least two more sittings. Bianca must be mistaken.

'Give me a moment,' I tell her.

As I find my shawl and put on my slippers again, I smile perversely at the thought of my father's anger when he sees Giacomo's shoddy workmanship, when he's brought back in disgrace and forced to explain himself. It will be no less than he deserves. I expect to hear my father's roar of fury with each step.

I pad barefoot down the corridor to the atrium and find Father already there. Between us is a stand, on which I can see the back of the canvas.

'Father?' I say.

My father stares at the painting. There are no furrows in his brow and he seems quite calm. I think he may even be smiling.

'Come,' he says tenderly. 'Come around here and see how the boy has captured you.'

My chest swells with nausea. I walk round, giving the painting a wide berth, to where my father stands. The whole world holds its breath with me.

I blink slowly, then open my eyes.

'How about it?' says my father.

I gasp – for it's an astonishing thing that I see. The painting is radiant, and perfect in every detail. I step closer to examine every curve and detail. My fingernails, the colour and shadows of my collarbone, the blue of my eyes, the tumble of my hair. The shape of my eyebrows, the tilt of my head, the shimmer of the sunshine on my skin. How can he have caught the colours and arcs of me like this without having me in front of him? The paint is still wet, unvarnished, and seems like some living thing. The bodice of my mother's dress sits lower on my chest than I remember, and there's a defiance in my look that must be an echo of my disposition when we parted. And there's something else, that's impossible to explain, and I feel myself blushing angrily at the thought. Because anyone looking at this picture might suspect that its creator knew more about me than I do of myself.

Faustina and Bianca scurry in to see as well. They clasp their hands together and gasp in delighted unison. They don't see the insolence of the brush strokes.

'Yes,' says my father, 'it is indeed a good likeness. I suppose he deserves his fee. Faustina, go to the courtyard and give him this.' He hands her a puckered purse.

'But he's already gone,' I say, taking Bianca's word for it.

'No such luck!' jokes my father. 'Workmen never forget what they're owed. No, he's waiting out there, on Beatrice's bench.'

Before anyone decides otherwise, I've snatched the purse from a startled Faustina.

'Here, I'll take it to him,' I say, and I march out to the courtyard.

My cheeks are burning. I will confront him. I'll tell him that I never want him to come near this house again or to paint any more pictures of me or to send me misleading gifts of pretend concern and care.

He's sitting where my father said he was, his arms stretched across the back of the bench, his leather-booted feet planted firmly on the ground. When he sees me he stands up.

'Laura! Thank you. Thank you for coming out. Please sit with me. I very much need to talk to you.'

I don't sit. My lips tremble no matter how much I wish they wouldn't.

'Do not call me by that name. I'm Signorina della Scala, and you . . . you're just a painter boy my father paid to do a job.'

I throw the purse on the bench.

He doesn't even look at it. He stares at me.

'But Laura . . .'

'Stop it! You have no right. It's wrong of you.'

'I've lost all sense of what is right and what is wrong,' he sighs.

'Then let me put you straight. I don't want anything to do with you. I want you to stay away from here. The painting is finished, and you have been paid in full. There's no reason for you to come back.'

'Yes, there is,' he says. 'And it's the best reason of all.'

I place both hands on my hips, as I've seen Faustina do with the drunken beggars who parade the streets. 'Oh, yes?'

'Laura, Beatrice and I weren't lovers. I promise you.'

His broad smooth hand is splayed against his chest, crushing his soft white shirt. His eyes are candid, the colour of burnished hazel. I can't look at them, or I am lost.

The bells of St Mark's start to chime, and I feel like my heart is keeping pace with them.

'You have until the ringing stops to explain yourself.'

Dong, goes the bell.

'She came to me. We'd met at the unveiling of an altarpiece in the church of San Marziale, by chance.'

Dong. I press my lips together, and look at the ground.

'I said I was a painter too, that's all.'

Dong. I stare at the strong lines of his shadow on the flag-stones.

'She wanted to learn. I wasn't sure at first – I warned her that people wouldn't approve. But she insisted.'

Dong.

'God, Laura, you must know how stubborn she can be!'

Dong.

He looks down for the fraction of a second, 'I mean, how stubborn she was.'

The sounds of the final chimes shiver above us, and he's silent. I turn around, so that he can't see the tears welling in my eyes. I *do* know how stubborn she was, and I remember her sketches as a girl. Of our mother, of the ships in the harbour, of me. The tears tumble out and slide down my face. I've been lied to so much, but the truth of his words shines brighter than the sun.

'I'll go,' he says quietly. I listen to his footsteps move away.

'Once she spent two days searching the streets for an amber necklace she had dropped,' I say. 'Everyone told her to give up. She sneaked out at night. When she came back she held it high above her head, like a trophy.'

He stops at the gate. When he turns towards me he grins. 'That sounds like her.'

We are silent again, standing facing one another.

'You know, all she ever did was talk about you,' he says. 'And in the end, before I'd even met you, you were all I ever talked about to her too.'

The wind whispers through the cypress trees. I think I hear someone crying, but it's a turtledove keening high above us. I can't speak.

'I think I was in love with you even before we met,' he says.

I stare at him. I don't move. I wonder if I've imagined his words. 'What did you say?'

'You're all I think about. I've tried not to. But Laura, I can't get you out of my head. I'll never be able to paint another picture again as long as I live. Unless it's a picture with you in it.'

His brown hands are splayed either side of him in a kind of entreaty. The pendant around his neck flashes suddenly and again it seems he might be an angel with speckles of paint on his arms.

We move towards each other. I reach up to his face and my hand looks pale against his brown skin. My fingers follow the subtle undulations of his deepening dimples, trace the prickle of his beard.

'Laura,' he says. The sound of his voice saying my name is like the taste of sweet wine – something rich and complicated that I've never had before. I tilt my face towards him and gently he touches my chin and moves me closer to him, in the same way he once, a whole day ago, moved it towards the sun.

He presses his lips up against mine, and they are parted, and he is kissing me.

31

There's a shriek and we break apart to see Faustina raising her hands in the air and then putting them over her mouth. She clatters down the steps towards us.

'Get away from her! Oh, Holy Madonna. Leave the poor girl alone. Don't you know she's a noblewoman? Laura, are you all right? What on earth has this man done to you?'

As she hurries towards us, Giacomo murmurs, 'You mustn't get into trouble. I won't cause any shame for you.'

'You couldn't do that if you tried,' I tell him. To Faustina, I say, 'Nothing's wrong – nothing at all!'

I hold Giacomo's hand. I will not let him go.

Faustina looks down at his tanned hand in my pale one. Her face changes; her brow furrows and her lips purse. I haven't seen her angry with me before.

'Dear God and all his holy saints! Your father chose badly when he picked Vincenzo, but do you suppose this servant boy is any better? Oh, Laura! If anyone had seen – your reputation would have been destroyed, like *that*.' She clicked her fingers. 'Beatrice will be turning in her grave to think of you throwing yourself away on this . . . this . . . *scoundrel*.' She slaps our hands apart, and points her stubby finger at Giacomo. 'And you! Playing with her affections. She's only just out of the convent. She doesn't understand. She does not know about such things.'

'Please, Faustina,' I say, but she narrows her eyes at Giacomo.

'Or did you really think she would cast her life out to sea with someone as lowly as you?'

'No, of course I don't, Signora,' he replies, backing away.

'A painter! Thank goodness I came when I did.' With her old hands she starts to bundle and push Giacomo down the garden path and towards the gates.

'I'll go,' he says, 'but I beg just a brief word with Laura.'

'Laura?' she says, her voice high-pitched at the monstrous use of my Christian name.

He walks around a speechlessly incensed Faustina and faces me again. His brow is heavy and sad. 'I'm sorry, Signorina della Scala, I'm sorry. It was quite wrong of me.'

I clutch his hands in my own.

'What's all this racket?' shouts my father. He strides out into the courtyard.

Our hands drop apart.

'Oh, nothing,' says Faustina. 'Laura has just paid the painter and he's about to leave. Isn't that right, Laura?'

I can't look at my father, but from the way he sucks the air in, I know he saw Giacomo and I touching.

'You impudent dog. Get off my property this instant.' His instructions squeeze out through the cracks of his gritted teeth. I dare a look and see that his face is as grey as stone.

'Please, Father –'

'Silence!' he bellows, and Faustina rocks on her heels.

'Sir,' begins Giacomo. 'Your daughter is not at fault here. I take . . .'

'Get out,' hisses my father, 'before I fetch my whip and beat you from here to Constantinople.'

Giacomo nods and backs off towards the gate. When he reaches it, he touches the tips of two fingers to his lips and looks at me. A tender, secret salute that pains and enchants me.

My father shouts after him. 'You'll never get another commission in all of Venice! Do you hear me, you insolent boy?'

They bundle me back into the house. I don't know what will happen next, but I feel strangely safe.

'It was the boy's fault,' Faustina says to my father.

'I know what happened. I saw the look in her eyes,' he snarls.

It's like I'm not there. And in some way, I'm not. I feel that nothing can touch me. I hear Giacomo's words, over and over. He said he loved me. And now, no matter how much they pull and drag at me, I know that I'm standing on something solid.

My father pulls me by the hand to his library, so that he can talk to me privately, but I see the familiar shadows at the crack under the door and I know Faustina and Bianca must crouch there, listening to us. It's like facing a bear in a cave, the way his voice echoes and clashes around the room.

'God in Heaven,' he rants. 'What on *earth* were you thinking?'

'I wasn't thinking at all,' I tell him, which is true. Something else was going on in the courtyard – something new, and not logical.

'That's perfectly clear,' he says, massaging his temples with his hands. 'Because you, young lady, were on the verge of ruining your life. Do you even realize what could have happened?' They're fatherly words: angry and fearful, but not completely malicious. 'And with Bianca in the house – the biggest gossip in all of Venice! Have you no *sense*? Who will marry a *painter's* hussy?'

He roams around me, striding like a miser whose treasure is at risk of being plundered. But I've had enough of being treated like just another currency in his chest.

'How can you lecture me?' I ask. 'You, whose only concern is for yourself and your political ambitions? If I didn't have any regard for this family's name, the name of my mother and the name of Beatrice, then do you think I would still be here?'

He stalls, speechless. I press on.

'So don't you take it on yourself to tell me how I should behave! Look at your own behaviour. What kind of father marries his daughter off to an old skeleton just for the sake of a seat on the Grand Council?'

His mouth grows wide in amazement. I don't care that his white-lipped fury has returned, or that the rest of his face looks like a swollen red pepper.

He draws his hand back and slaps my cheek. He isn't a strong man, but still my skin burns as I stand my ground.

'Go to your room,' he says under his breath.

My own breath comes in sharp bursts as the heat across my face subsides. I stare at him, hoping he sees the fire of defiance in my soul.

'Go to your room!' he bellows.

'I heard you the first time,' I reply, turning from him and walking as calmly as possible to the door.

Faustina sits at the end of my bed, wringing her hands. I curl up among the pillows. Birds are singing through the open window and the heavy evening sun has started to trickle in like honey.

'I'm so sorry, Laura.'

'It wasn't your fault,' I say.

'I should never have made such a fuss,' she says. 'If he hadn't heard me, he would never . . .'

'I know. You were just worried about me.'

'I've told Bianca not to breathe a word of this to anyone,' she adds.

'I feel like telling the whole of Venice,' I say, raising my head from the pillow and giving a weak smile.

Faustina shakes her head. 'Well, you're certainly not to do that. And besides, your father has instructed me to make sure you don't leave this room.'

She wags her finger and furrows her eyebrows in playful mockery of him. I laugh; at least Faustina and I are friends again.

'You'll have to stay here until he calms down. I'll bring your dinner up.' There's a knock at the front door and she bustles out.

I don't feel like eating. I don't want to sleep. I can't think of anything except what happened in the garden.

From being forced to marry a man I could never have loved, now I love a man whom I can never marry. I go to the window and lean out, catching my breath again, because it's at that moment I realize: I love him. I understand for the first time why people carve their names together on the trunks of cypress trees. I realize that love needs to be announced. And yet I can't announce mine. If my father has his way, I might never even see Giacomo again.

Faustina scurries back in.

'Allegreza is here,' she says.

'Again? What does she want?'

'Your father has asked her to take you to confession.'

'I have nothing to confess,' I say, indignant hackles rising.

'He's told her all about the painter.'

I snort, imagining Allegreza, of all people, sitting outside the confessional on cushions of hypocrisy, while I pour out my sins within. But I know that this isn't really why she's here.

Faustina smoothes out my hair with her hands and then draws it up into a tight knot, tying it fast with a ribbon so that I'll appear serious and repentant. After she's left the room, I take out my mask and slip it under my cape. After what's happened, I feel wild and reckless, I have nothing to lose. Allegreza stands waiting in the atrium, her features dark and shadowed.

'Laura,' she says gravely, nodding at my father. 'Come with me and all will be well.'

32

The sun finally vanishes over the horizon as Allegreza brings me to the cluster of gondolas at Mazzini.

'Where are you taking me?'

'You're a member,' she says simply, 'and there is a meeting.'

We sit in silence as the gondola takes twists and turns down back canals I have never seen before. When we climb out of the boat, we are somewhere that I don't recognize – in the east of the city and near the boatyards, if the ringing hammers are anything to go by. We walk quickly through the narrow alleys and reach a small, grey, angular chapel. Dozens of candles dance inside, and the masked women murmur quiet greetings to me. Others touch my hand or my shoulder in welcome.

I grow calmer. This has all the rhythms and sounds of an ordinary meeting of the Segreta. Perhaps that's all it is.

Allegreza walks slowly to the altar and the women settle into silence. She can always quieten a room with a single gesture.

Two other women coax a small, pale, pretty girl to the centre of the glimmering chapel. She has smooth fair hair and large brown eyes, timid and trembling.

'Welcome, Cecile,' says Allegreza. 'This is the Society of Secrets and you must tell us yours.'

The women are still. I want to comfort this girl who looks so frightened. In a lyrical, throaty voice, and a faltering Italian softened and liquefied by an accent that I half recognize, she speaks.

'And you will help me?' she asks. 'I was told you could help with my beloved. He's no soldier, and shouldn't be made to fight.'

'If your secret is worthy, we can arrange his exemption.'

'My secret is worthy,' says Cecile. 'It concerns the Doge of Venice.'

Murmurs ripple around the room. They must be wondering, like me, if this is a secret they've heard before.

The girl holds her head up and raises her voice a little. 'Well, it's really a secret about his son.'

I feel Paulina stiffen at my side. 'A secret about Nicolo?' she asks anxiously.

'Not Nicolo,' says Cecile. 'The other son, Roberto. The one who's supposed to be dead.'

Supposed? There's no more murmuring, and the silence is profound, although some of the women throw glances in Grazia's direction. Her eyes flicker behind her cat's mask, but she doesn't speak.

Cecile looks nervously over at Allegreza, who nods slightly. 'Go on.'

'I wish to tell you that the Doge's firstborn son is alive.'

The women break out in a disbelieving chorus.

'She lies to the Segreta!' shouts one.

'She plays us false!' cries another. 'It's not true.'

'I've seen him with my own eyes,' Cecile insists, raising her voice about the hubbub. 'In Paris.'

Allegreza strides up to the girl, and the masked women fall silent again. 'This is a serious declaration,' says Allegreza. 'The boy's bones rest in a tomb in this very city.'

Cecile's face creases. 'What can I say? He spoke to me of his childhood, and of the vendetta that drove him away. He was injured with a sword and spent many weeks recovering.'

Though she's still frightened, her tone is forthright. She holds out her palms to show that she has nothing to conceal. There is no hint of guile in her eyes.

Many of the women rush to gather around Grazia, who leans heavily on one of them. They fan her, while someone runs to fetch a stool for her to sit on. 'He's alive?' she mutters. 'My son's killer lives? And in Paris?' She sounds disorientated, made almost drunk by the news.

'Not in Paris any more,' says Cecile. 'He's returned to Venice.'

Grazia wails and slumps against her neighbour in a faint. Allegreza calls for silence. 'We can't know yet if this is the truth. I'll question Cecile further, and we shall reconvene.'

Paulina tugs at my arm, and pulls me into a corner. Behind her mask, her eyes have widened with fear. 'It's not true,' she says.

'This girl has no reason to lie,' I say as gently as I can.

'Do you see what this means?' she says.

My attention is on the women reviving Grazia, and I shake my head.

'If Roberto is still alive, then my Nicolo is no longer the first son.'

My head snaps round to her in shock. 'Even though he's not the heir, he's still a fine husband.'

'He's not the man I thought he was.'

'But you told me you loved him – with or without his fortune.'

She sighs. 'Well, yes, but it's not as simple as that.'

She's deflated, and walks away towards the door. Grazia has risen from the bench, waving away the supporting hands of the other women.

'Allegreza, may I talk to the girl?'

Allegreza nods, and Cecile looks terrified as Grazia moves towards her, the skirts of her black mourning gown swaying.

'There's no need to fear us,' Grazia says, 'as long as you're telling the truth.'

'Please . . . I only . . . I can't tell you any more.'

'When it comes to secrets, there's always more to tell. First, how did you meet the man you claim is Roberto?'

'He trained with my brother,' she says, 'two years ago, in Paris. He confided in him, and that is how I came to know of it.'

'Trained at what profession?' asks Grazia.

'As a painter,' says the girl.

I tingle under my mask. I put a steadying hand against a pillar.

Grazia looks at the girl and says, 'So this is hearsay, unsubstantiated, from a brother whom we can't question.'

'My brother is no more a liar than I am,' says Cecile. 'He

says that Roberto wears a pendant, engraved with the Doge's crest. He never takes it off.'

I'm suddenly cold as the doubts seep through my pores. My painter, with his curls and his soft eyes, is the Doge's firstborn. Giacomo is Roberto. His bones do not lie under the porphyry slab in St Mark's, for there's flesh on them still. Flesh that I've touched. Breath that has intertwined with my own.

And now I think about how I saw the Duchess smile at him during the hunt. I think about what the Doge said about his talents. I think about the way Giacomo fumbled with the pendant around his neck when we talked about the old days. All is not what it seems. Trust no one in Venice. There are no friends. These parts of my catechism are roaring in my head. But suddenly I know something. I won't listen to the doubts that have been planted by the voices of other people. I'll listen to my heart.

I take off the suffocating mask and drop it to the ground.

Grazia's questions continue, and for each Cecile has a ready answer. I can see Carina's mother hardening like stone. Her resolve is gathering like a great wave, fuelled by indignation at a debt she thought paid long ago, but paid in counterfeit coin.

'His blood belongs to my family,' she whispers gravely.

'But, that's foolish!' I blurt out. 'The vendetta was years ago. Roberto's a man now. If he's even alive.'

Now the women turn to me. My naked face.

'My husband would claim those years were not his to spend,' says Grazia.

I make a conscious effort to quell the roar of my thoughts.

I have to find him. I have to warn him. If they would kill an eleven-year-old boy, a man is nothing.

'Excuse me,' I say, pushing past the woman.

'Where are you going?' someone calls.

'We counsel you,' says another, grabbing me by the arm. 'Do not break the vows of the Segreta.'

I can't break free from her long-nailed talons. But Allegreza looks down calmly and says, 'Let her go. We can't hold her here.'

Lifting my skirts, I dash out of the door and down the front steps. I leave the buzz and the scramble of the women behind me. I must find him.

33

I'm grateful that the anonymous cloak I wore to the meeting will go some way to disguise me on this journey.

A gondola wobbles in the water, its pilot fanning his face with his broad hat.

'Please! Please, sir, take me to the Lido. I need to get to the artisan quarter.'

He holds out his hand to help me aboard. 'I'll get you there as fast as I can. Sit, and catch your breath.'

I do my best to keep calm and think logically. Giacomo's secret has followed him across Europe like a lingering infection for which there's no cure. His death warrant is signed and he doesn't know it, but neither do many others. There is still time.

As we drift behind a low warehouse, the gondolier wants to know where exactly to leave me. I feel a lurch of panic when I realize that I don't know.

'Do you know a man called Giacomo?' I ask, a foolish frightened question, born of desperation.

'I know several men of that name,' he smiles.

There's a choke in my voice. 'He's a painter. Do you know *anyone* who I can ask?'

The gondolier steps out of his boat and takes me by the hand as I jump off. 'Wait here a moment, Signorina, I'll see if I can find out.'

He walks away off into a dark lane telling me he'll be back and it's better if he goes alone. But I can't just stand waiting for him. I have to run.

Three ragged boys dangle their feet in the water and I rush towards them.

'Do you know Giacomo?' I ask. They look at me and giggle.

My gondolier comes whistling down the lane in a slow saunter. He seems surprised by my haste as I run over the cobbles.

'The baker says he knows an artist called Giacomo,' he says. 'Lives on Caligari, at number seventeen. Go to the end of this bank, take the lane that curves into the left, and walk until you get to Fellucci. Caligari is the third on the right.'

I thank him over my shoulder as I run. My feet slap out a frantic beat.

At Caligari, I slow, scanning up and down. What if he isn't even here? Perhaps he has a commission elsewhere. A sudden image of him, paint-stained and whistling like a free boy, comes to mind. But he's not free any more.

My fists feel like lumps of marble as I lift both my arms and bang hard on the door to number seventeen.

'Giacomo!'

Silence.

Please be here, I pray.

Annalena used to tell me that desperate prayers sometimes carry a fierce and exceptional power. I never used to believe her, but in this instance it is so. The door swings open.

'Laura!' he smiles, and I can't speak. His face creases into a frown. There in the doorstep with my heavy breath and my fearsome beating heart, he wraps his arms around me and I cling to him. 'Whatever's the matter?' he asks.

'You're in danger,' I say.

He chuckles. 'Your father?'

'The de Ferraras. The vendetta.'

That silences his laughter, and his face drains of colour. His lips open a fraction. 'Come inside.'

He weaves his fingers among mine. The narrow wooden stairs creak as we climb. At the top is a planked, crooked-looking door. He pushes it open with his boot and pulls me inside. He lifts a bundle of my hair and buries his face in it and breathes in.

The room is simple and bright – illuminated by two skylights, both open to the elements. A plain table stands in the middle of the floor, covered with books, sketches, notes and canvases, and a cot with tangled sheets is pushed into the corner. Paints and frames and easels fill the space on the other side. There's a simple wardrobe beside the bed.

'You know?' he says.

I touch his chest with my fingertips and loosely he puts his hand over mine. I lift the chain that hangs around his neck. I drape the gold pendant over my hand and look at it very closely. I see it. The Ducal crest.

'Roberto.'

He's wrapped a blanket over me, for even with the heat I'm shivering. He crouches by his small stove as I pace the room, trying to explain what I know. For the second time, I break the oath of the Segreta. A tiny kettle bubbles on the fire and spills steam over its edge. With a cloth he picks it out and pours hot water into two cups on the dresser. His hand trembles.

'You could have told me,' I say.

He comes to me again and hangs his head down on to my shoulder, and I hear his breathing.

'It's been so long since someone called me by that name,' he says. 'I never wanted to deceive you.'

'I understand,' I say, 'but now others know too. Grazia will surely tell her husband.'

'We don't know that. It's possible that the news may not have spread beyond the women there today. They *are* the Society of Secrets, after all.' He speaks with a composure that makes me feel I will faint.

'It isn't worth the risk,' I reply. 'You have to get away from here.'

He sits and digs his elbows into the table, holding his head.

'I've spent so long running away.'

A sharp rapping on the door makes us jump.

'It's them!' I say. 'They've come already!'

'Stop worrying so much,' he whispers and touches my face. 'Not even the gossips of Venice could mobilize everyone that quickly. But whoever it is might be looking for you, and you mustn't be found here.'

He pours away one of the cups of tea, and opens the old oak doors of the wardrobe that stands on the opposite wall. It's full of his clothes: soft white shirts, black cotton trousers and two jackets, one with a missing button. A pair of leather boots.

'Please be careful,' I say, stepping inside.

He kisses me on the lips as the visitor below knocks once more. Then he closes the door, leaving me in a blanket of darkness with only the smell of him. There's a thin strip of light where the doors meet. I lean against the crack and stare.

First I hear a woman's muffled voice, but there in this enclosed space, and with my mind swimming, I can't tell whose it is. Has Grazia come alone? I hear footsteps, but no panic in them. Then a figure enters the room.

She wears a black cloak, and stands facing away from me. Roberto is opposite, with a look of confusion on his face. As the woman draws down her hood, the shock of her red-gold hair tumbles free.

'Hello, Carina,' says Roberto.

34

Grazia's daughter titters, and her profile catches in the light.

'Well, well,' she says. 'Where have *you* been hiding?'

'I've been painting,' he says guardedly.

'Hiding in plain sight,' she says. 'I see now why I never spotted it. You've changed so much.'

'Did your mother tell you?' he asks.

'She's in quite a fluster,' says Carina. 'But why didn't *you* tell me you were back in Venice? How did you expect me to recognize you in these clothes, doing this job, living this life? I consider it most unfriendly of you.'

If she has found him, I'm thinking, *others can too.*

'A lot has happened since we were children,' he replies. 'You know I couldn't have come back without a disguise.' He sweeps his hand around as if everything there explains what he means.

She walks towards the wardrobe. I freeze, with my eye pressed to the crack, and she seems to look right at me, but I see from her solemn face that she doesn't.

'The curse of childhood,' she mutters. 'I can help you, Roberto. That is why I'm here. I know how you could come back into society. I have a way.'

'I don't think it's possible,' he says. He watches Carina closely, his hands at his side, neither comfortable nor relaxed.

Carina, with her back to him still, smiles. 'Imagine being able to hold your head up high as the son of the Doge. Imagine walking around St Mark's in your fine clothes, with everyone knowing who you are, never having to look over your shoulder again.'

'I don't know,' he says. 'There's a lot to be said for the life of an anonymous painter.' He glances over to where I'm hiding. I'm holding my chest, trying to calm my breathing.

Carina looks around his simple room. I think I see a little sneer. Whatever it is, it crumples her smooth face, and makes her look ugly for a second. 'You really think there's merit in living here? Like this? Surrounded by peasants?'

He digs his fists into his hips in the way I've seen before. 'It's not for everyone, I admit.'

'All I have to do is say the word,' she says. 'All I have to do is talk to my father. Then you'll have freedom *and* power. No one will care about that stupid vendetta any more. For goodness' sake, it's all such a long time ago. I can't even remember who started it. Anyway, I would be able to convince them how meaningless it is.'

As I watch, she takes a few steps towards him and places her hand carefully on his shoulder. His eyes settle on her fingers.

'I fear even your charms aren't that great, Carina.'

'What happened to our friendship?' she asks. 'I thought I would've been the first person you'd look for when you came back.'

'It was difficult.'

He steps away, but she moves closer to him again.

'I thought we were going to be more than friends. I was sure. We were only just old enough for love when the terrible fight happened, and everything changed.'

'We were only children,' he says.

'I thought you were dead.' She touches his chest, softly this time, and I wish she wouldn't. Her hand trails down across his stomach. 'If I'd known that you were alive all these years . . . why, I would have . . .'

She lifts his shirt up slowly, and I hold my breath. He lets her do it, and inch by inch his torso is exposed. A wide, jagged-looking scar stretches almost completely across the left side of his tanned chest, stopping near his heart.

'Carina, stop,' he says, pulling away.

'Oh, come, Roberto,' she says, 'I'm just looking.' She brushes his chest and places her hand flat upon it. His back is against the crooked door. I can only watch. 'They said no one could survive that wound.'

'What are you doing here, Carina?' his voice is thick, and his Adam's apple bobs in his throat.

'I'm here,' she sighs, 'because I have a secret too.'

'Yes?' he says, smoothing his shirt down.

Carina turns away again, and lowers her eyes to the floor.

'If you want to know the truth, I've actually known about your being here for months,' she says. 'I've just been biding my time. Waiting for this chance to talk to you.'

I can't see her eyes. Is she lying?

Roberto frowns, clearly as confused as me. 'Who told you?'

'A-ha,' she says. 'You must know. Think about it.'

For a long time there's silence. Roberto looks straight at me, then says quietly, 'Beatrice.'

'Women can't keep secrets,' laughs Carina. 'Didn't you know that?'

'Then she trusted you with a grave secret,' says Roberto.

'And I never told anyone,' says Carina. 'Though I could have.'

'I sincerely hope that is true,' he says.

Carina seems to ignore this. 'And now I've heard,' she says, 'that you're close to the other sister. I'm sure you already know of her grasping father's foul, territorial temper.'

Her tone drips with contempt. She looks at him with satisfaction and anticipation. She seems swollen with a kind of power.

'I want you to leave,' he says, moving towards the door.

A ripple of fresh affection sweeps over me. I want to be out there, standing by his side.

'Beatrice was a fool,' continues Carina. 'And Laura is no better.'

The transformation has happened before my eyes. Carina, stripped of her loveliness, spits out her words brutally.

'Beatrice was my friend,' says Roberto. 'And her sister is far more.'

Carina rounds on him with a brittle laugh. 'Far more?'

'Yes. Far more. I love Laura della Scala, and I think that she loves me too.'

Carina's body stiffens.

'Don't speak like a fool, Roberto. Laura is nothing but a convent girl. Unrefined. Ignorant. *Inexperienced*. She can't satisfy a Doge's son.'

'She's the most beautiful woman in Venice,' he says. 'The fear that I am not good enough for her is all that haunts me now.'

'Well, if that's all you're frightened of, then you're more of a fool than I thought,' she snaps. But her body changes; she runs a hand through her hair and her voice becomes softer, honeyed, heavy. 'I'm a widow. I'm free – and I can set you free too.' She reaches for him again, but he pushes her hand away.

'No,' he says, opening the door to let her out.

'Don't you find me attractive?' she simpers. 'Don't you think we'd make a fine Venetian pair?'

'Please go, Carina.'

She's flushed. She steps from him and brushes down her dress. She takes two deep breaths, then shakes her locks back over her shoulder.

'Fine,' she says. 'I will give you time. There are men all over this city who would chop off their own arms for my hand in marriage. Think on it, then send me your answer.'

She sweeps away. I hear the pressure of her slow steps on the staircase, and finally the slam of the outside door. He comes back over to the wardrobe and throws it open. Our lips meet with me still half standing inside, and his hands on my waist lift me out. He carries me over to the tousled bed.

'Beatrice never told me,' I say, still a little angry that this is another secret.

'I asked her not to tell anyone. I let my mask slip in a moment of weakness. She was so kind-hearted, I never dreamt she might tell someone else.'

'She trusted Carina. So did I.'

On the narrow bed, I rest my head on Roberto's chest, and slide my hand under his loose shirt. He shivers a little as the smoothness of his skin gives way to the rough tissue of the scar.

'Did it hurt?'

'I hardly remember,' he says. 'We were fishing, my friend and I, just after dawn. We didn't see the men until they were close by. Didn't see the swords they held until it was too late. I thought that I'd been shoved, that's all, and fell into the water. But there was a lot of blood.'

I let my hand trace the line of his ribs. 'Poor you. Only eleven years old.'

'Julius's men left me for dead, and my friend rushed for help. I don't remember being fished out or taken back to the palazzo. A fever set in later, but after I'd recovered they sent me away at once with Mathieu. He looked after me for years in Paris.'

'So the tomb in the chapel . . .?'

'Empty. My mother insisted on a closed coffin, claiming I'd received a terrible injury to my face too. Only a handful of my father's most loyal subjects know the truth.'

I prop myself up on my elbow, and look into his eyes. He tries to kiss me, but I place a hand on his chest. 'You must consider Carina's offer.'

His eyes widen. 'Why?'

'If Julius would attack an innocent boy, he'll come after an innocent man just as surely. Marrying Carina is the only way of putting a stop to all this.'

'Is that what you want?' he asks me. 'Please don't tell me that's what you want me to do.'

'Of course it's not. But this is your *life* we're talking about.'

'Laura, if I married that woman, I would never breathe a single happy breath again as long as I lived.'

'But if you don't marry her, you can't stay in Venice.'

I know it's more serious than that; if he doesn't marry her, he won't be safe anywhere in the world. Carina has him in checkmate. Now she waits for him to consider his options, and to realize that there's no choice.

'But if I marry her,' he says, 'then I won't be able to do this.' He brushes his lips against my collarbone. 'Or this.' He kisses my lips. 'I'd never even be able to hold these hands in mine ever again.'

His touch sends a thrill across my skin, and I don't want him to stop. But through the veil of passion, a darker shadow lurks.

'Someone is going to kill you,' I say, my voice a soft whisper. 'They could be coming for you at this very moment.'

He kisses me again, and tells me everything is going to be all right.

'My mother used to say that,' I tell him. 'And she was wrong.'

'Right,' he says, springing up off the bed. 'I'll tell you what I'll do.'

He strides over to his little desk, laying out his plan. He's going to write to Carina, and tell her how things are. That they cannot be together because he doesn't feel for her as a lover. Then, when she's pacified, he's going to talk to Julius himself, man to man, and persuade him that the vendetta has no value any more. That it will serve no purpose. I'm not sure, and tell him so, but he insists he will try. His confidence carries me with it.

'What about your parents?' I say, remembering that night at the palace when Julius and Grazia were turned away. 'Your father has kept the pretence well. Too well, perhaps. Julius will be furious.'

'As far as my father was concerned, for many years I was as good as dead. I never saw either of my parents for over eight years.'

'But –'

'No buts,' he says. 'Julius is an old man now. His grief is old and well-worn. He will understand.'

He slides a drawer out and rummages in it. He presses flat a piece of creamy parchment and dips a quill into a little pot of black ink. I watch as he writes his note of refusal. He says he's going to fetch his friend Mathieu, who will take the message to Carina.

'Don't be mad,' I plead with him again. 'Stay here.'

Roberto smiles at me. 'I'll be back soon,' he says, 'and I'll bring a bottle of Vin Santo to celebrate.'

'Celebrate what?'

'Everything. Life. Liberty. Love.'

The hour that I wait is a torment unlike any I've suffered. I imagine him dragged away, or worse, bleeding by the side of a street with my name on his lips. But soon I hear his feet pounding up the stairs and he bursts into the room with a smile on his face, holding a bottle by the neck. We embrace, and he twirls me round.

'It's done,' he says. 'She'll have the note by now.'

He tips the wine, and we drink from the same glass. The

taste is sweet and rich, and it blunts the sense of dread. Perhaps every day will be like this soon.

'I'll go and see your father tomorrow,' Roberto announces.

'What on earth for?' I ask.

His face is suddenly solemn. 'Well . . . to tell him of my intentions. Unless . . .'

I put a finger to his lips, laughing. 'I'm joking, silly.'

He smiles too, and tries to bite at my finger, then plants soft kisses along the inside of my arm that set me giggling because they tickle.

This thing that is happening to us, so deep and precious, is seeping into my bones. And I already feel I'm going to lose it, and that there'll be no way, then, to get it back.

'Do you think he'll give his permission?' asks Roberto.

I can't imagine my father's face when he discovers the insolent painter boy is the Doge's son. I wonder what he would do. Bow and scrape? Fall to his knees?

'Once he's picked himself off the floor!' I reply. 'The rest of the Grand Council will have been informed before sunset, if I know my father.'

His lips taste of the sweet wine. As we break apart, his eyes are grave.

'Beatrice missed you a great deal,' he said. 'She would be happy for us.'

Coming from his mouth, my sister's name sounds like a secret wish. Roberto dries my eyes with his lips. 'I'm sorry,' he says, 'I've made you sad.'

'No, it's not that,' I say. 'I think you were the only thing that made her happy, near to the end.'

It's not the time to talk to him about the certainty that festers within me, about the violence of her death. I look away. He sees so much when he looks at me.

It's getting dark and there's a thudding at the door once more. Even without seeing the visitor, I know it's a man.

'Mathieu!' Roberto says.

'I'll go,' I say, and before he can stop me, I rush down the stairs in my bare feet and unlatch the door. Standing there is a grim, thick-browed, grey-faced man, who is definitely not Mathieu. He asks for Roberto in a mumble, his mouth hidden behind a filthy scarf. There's something about him that makes me shudder. I know him from somewhere and a flicker of instinct sharpens me.

'Roberto's not here,' I lie.

'Then give him this,' the man says, and he holds out a small box the size of my hand. 'It's from Carina de Ferrara.'

I have questions for Carina, but I will keep them to myself. The grey face seems, in any case, to be closed to interrogation.

I carry the box back upstairs and put it on the table. Roberto, seeing my expression, is quickly at my side. He slides his arm around me.

'What is it?' he asks.

'From Carina.'

I open the box, and there's a piece of muslin cloth inside, tied with knotted string. Roberto goes to a drawer and comes back with a knife. I notice there's a red stain seeping through the muslin.

Roberto takes it out, and slices through the string. He pulls the sides apart slowly. His face darkens.

'What is it?'

'Look away,' he says.

The air sweeps in and out of his mouth. Something scares him now and his fear touches me also, because up until this moment, he's just laughed in the face of danger, and his laughter was like a rock to which I've been clinging.

'What has she sent you?' I ask him but he says nothing, instead replacing the muslin package in the box, and taking a folded piece of paper from within. A note.

'Roberto?'

His silence is terrifying. He reads the missive to himself.

'No!' he moans. 'No, no.'

'My darling?' I ask. 'What is it?'

With both hands balled into fists on the table, he hangs his head. I'm shocked when a tear splashes on the stained wood.

I don't want to touch the box, so I walk around the table to stand beside him, and peer inside. Inside the cloth lies a flaccid piece of bloodied meat, pink at the tip and discoloured at the thick root. It takes hardly any time at all to realize that it's a human tongue.

35

I slam closed the box and take Roberto in my arms. Horror holds us in a wider embrace.

'Mathieu?' I ask.

'Read the note,' says Roberto. I take it from his loose grasp. Blood smears the bottom edge of the page.

> *Dear Roberto,*
> *You sent me a poisoned message, so I cut out the poisoned flesh. I*
> *hope you will find it a mercy that your friend feels pain no longer,*
> *resting as he does, at the bottom of the lagoon.*
>
> *To spare any further agony for either of us, grant me your*
> *presence at the engagement of your brother and Paulina. There we*
> *shall announce our love to all.*
>
> *In eternity,*
> *Yours, Carina*

'I'll pursue her,' he says, bowed and broken. 'I'll have justice!'

I cradle his head. 'No, please. Look what she's capable of. Look what she's just done.'

'She's killed Mathieu.'

'I know,' I say. 'All the more reason why we have to keep you safe.'

My instincts have been right. His choices sharpen in front of me. To get out of Venice now, and hope that this vicious evil won't pursue him. Or to stay. Stay and marry Carina to end the vendetta and save his life.

He holds me as if he's never going to let me go.

The evening chill enters the room, and our conversation is like a siege, albeit with two lovers facing each other unwillingly. As many times as I advance with the same cold logic – that he must do as Carina says – so many times he resists. He responds with kisses, but his defences and his reasoning are weakening. The frailty of their foundations is exposed. Love is not enough, and we both see it. And now, with each kiss, I can feel the acceptance of his heart as it retreats further inside its walls. The closer we come to the inevitable conclusion, the further we are pushing each other away.

'Your life is in her hands,' I say, not for the first time. 'She can crush it with a word.'

That's the power of a secret, I almost add.

'I'd rather die than marry her,' he says.

That makes me sit up, if not in anger, then in angry love. 'Don't speak like that! Don't you dare. You have no right.'

He thumbs the tears from my eyes. 'Forgive me.'

'You wouldn't only be marrying her for yourself,' I say. 'But for me too.'

The perversity of my words doesn't escape me.

'If I do . . . if I marry her . . .' he says, 'then I will still see you.'

I nod, trying not to cry again. I know he's lying, and I love him wretchedly for it. Carina won't let us near each other.

'We must be strong,' I say.

'And you must go now,' he says, 'before you are missed.'

All my limbs are heavy as I take my leave. There are no more decisions to be made. When I reach the door, I look back up. He presses two fingers to his lips. Before stepping out into the street, I gather my grief around me like a shroud.

The feeling of his lips against mine stays with me on the walk home. Long after I've left his studio; long after I've arrived back to my father's crumbling house; long after I've peeled off my clothes and slipped into my bed. After all of this, I dream of his lips on mine.

For the next two days, I rarely come out of my room. Faustina's footsteps get faster up and down the corridors. Her feet have always absorbed her anxiety, while the rest of her body behaves as though it's business as usual. I smell breakfast, and dinner, and supper as the hours pass. I hear her answering the door. I hear her shouting at Bianca. But her feet give her away. She's worrying about me. There's nothing she can do for her Laura now. And though she can irritate like the nettles of Hell, as people you love sometimes do, she's been a mother and a friend to me. Under Faustina's stern mask is an ocean of kindness. I believe in her.

Who else can I believe in? Paulina – she's worn a mask since the moment we met. The Segreta? I nearly believed in those women too, but not any more. And Carina. How could I have looked into her face so many times and not have seen the dreadful evil lurking there?

I take out the carved bird Roberto made for me. It's something from another age, a time before my eyes were opened.

Faustina brings a note and she's full of hope. 'Perhaps it's something good,' she suggests and hovers as I pull it open.

> Laura,
> You are no longer welcome to the wedding party of Paulina and Nicolo. Do not shame yourself by attempting to come. I trust this is clear.
>   Carina

My laughter is bitter.

'What is it, what does it say?' asks Faustina.

I throw it on the chair, grateful that Faustina can't read. I think of the other note with Mathieu's blood smeared across it.

'It's not important,' I say. 'But I feel ready for some food.'

'Thank goodness,' says Faustina, bustling out of the room. To make Faustina happy, all you have to do is tell her you're hungry.

After she's gone, I retrieve the letter and read it again. Until that moment I hadn't been planning to attend: I couldn't think of facing the world and its painted faces, the constructed jollity of a wedding. But this note, with its terse presumption, makes something else rise within me. One way or another, Carina's told me what to do since I met her that night at the Doge's party. Well, I was a different person then, and I won't be told what to do any more.

Faustina arrives with a plate of bread, cold meats, pickles

and cheese. There are figs and dates, and an orange in slices. It's enough to feed a household and the sight of it makes me laugh.

'What is it?' she asks, affronted.

'Nothing. I'm just wondering what on earth I shall wear to Nicolo and Paulina's wedding.'

'You're going then?' she frowns.

'Of course I am.'

36

I wear a simple silk dress of cream and green. Ceremonial enough to fit in at a gathering like this, but not so spectacular that I'll draw unwanted attention. I need to stay in the background. The party is at a mansion on the north shore that belongs to the Doge and will now pass to his son. I see the same pageant of bedecked nobles as before: women with faces so white they might be alabaster come to life; men full to the brim with self-satisfaction. Most step out of their own boats. Others trot from the horse carriages, tossing instructions at their long-suffering drivers. The familiar noises and shouts of a party like this are like an assault. Guests are welcomed by lute and harpsichord. I see Carina, but only the flash of her face and her red-gold hair through the crowd. I raise my fan and duck out of sight. Of Giacomo . . . of Roberto, rather, there is no sign.

A lush carpet of deep red stretches from the great stone archway through which the guests pour, chattering, to the inside of Nicolo's majestic home. Men greet each other with bulky handshakes. Women cluster in prim little groups, chirping and squeaking at one another.

A gong sounds, and the guests are led down a gallery lined with stained glass, and into an adjoining chapel that's attached to Nicolo's grand house. I see Paulina in the distance, with a colourful gaggle of girls and women flapping around her. Her maid of honour carries the jewelled bridal chalice.

There was a time, not so long ago, when I would have been thrilled by the sights and sounds of such a gathering. Today I feel nothing but the bitter turning of my stomach. I stand behind a pillar, staying back. Even my father doesn't know I've come.

Nicolo and Paulina are led on to a ribboned platform by the stooped old bishop, a cousin of the Doge himself. Paulina's beautiful in pearly white and a sparkling veil. Nicolo smiles solemnly in a thick silk suit of indigo. Each of them is kissed by the Duchess and the Doge. Paulina's uncle looks on, dabbing his eyes from time to time and nodding at the well-wishers.

The music stops, and the mitred bishop begins with a Latin benediction. He follows with the sacred words on the dissolubility of the marriage bonds, on fidelity. He speaks of conforming the church's laws, and finally, if a little stuffily, on the subject of love. Paulina and Nicolo cannot take their eyes off each other, and for a moment, even my own cares seem a little lighter.

With the ceremony completed, the promises given, the party swells with anticipation. Just as the guests begin to break up for the banquet in the main hall, the gong chimes once more.

The surprised crowd watches as Carina steps out on to the platform. The bishop himself is goggle-eyed. Her gown is white and gold, with skirts more voluminous and luxurious than Paulina's. An extravagant collar of diamonds lies against her throat.

'Ladies and gentlemen of Venice,' she says. 'Welcome to this wonderful day.' The crowd murmurs, partly in agreement and partly in confusion, but they let her continue as she congratulates the bride and groom. Momentarily, she looks unsure of herself, and says quietly, 'I have another announcement.'

Heads in the crowd move closer together, the better to exchange their hushed exclamations of uncertainty.

'What's she on about?' I hear a man whisper to his wife.

Carina claps her hands together to beckon a fresh silence and raises her voice.

'For many years, two of the leading families of this city have suffered under a pall of mourning. One of those families is my own. I don't have to speak of what has come before – it saddens me, as it should sadden all who value innocent life.'

Julius, standing close to the centre of the chapel, has turned crimson. Grazia holds on to her husband's arm and I see she's working hard to contain what boils inside him, patting his arm, hushing him. I wonder what, if anything, she knew of her daughter's plan. I can't see the Doge and the Duchess Besina, but I see other heads turned towards them, watching for their reaction too.

Carina looks sideways. 'In the name of love, and forgiveness, I introduce you to my future husband.' Some of the onlookers try to initiate a ripple of applause, but it doesn't catch on. 'Come out, Roberto.'

The murmurs in the crowd grow louder and I see him. He

walks stiffly from the side of the altar, his face pale and serious. Carina holds her hand out to him.

I can't look, but I must. I thought that I could cope with seeing this, that my love was strong enough.

'Roberto?' says a voice in the crowd. 'What are you doing?'

It's the Doge.

Roberto's name is suddenly on everyone's lips. There are gasps, cries of disbelief. Carina's face widens in ostentatious pleasure. I watch Roberto take her hand. He who has kissed me, stroked my hair, touched my face. Her face looks hard even when she's smiling and so does her hand, laden as it is with rings. It must be a cold thing for him to hold.

A terrible commotion ensues. I see the Duchess run towards her son, terrified now that he's been revealed. She stands in front of him, her eyes burning, as if ready to protect him from attack.

The crowd frays around the edges. 'The Doge's son lives!'

The stooped bishop ineffectually tries to encourage people to take their seats again. The sea of people has parted, and on one side the Duchess stands with Roberto, Carina and the Doge. On the other Julius and Grazia glower, flanked by those loyal to them. It's a dangerous sight and there is anger in the room that can be measured by the heat that rises from both sides.

Carina steps in front of Roberto. 'There's no need for confusion or chaos,' she says.

'Do you think, child,' Julius spits in a low growl, 'that I will stand for this marriage after all that has happened to our family?'

'Father, please,' Carina responds. 'There's no sense in this. We love one another.'

It looks as though Julius is too angry to speak. His chest rises and falls.

'Would you kill my husband?' Carina presses.

'He's not your husband yet,' her father replies.

'But we are promised to each other,' says Carina. 'Tell them, Roberto. Tell them all.'

Julius shakes his head, but the crowd looks on hungrily.

Roberto steps forward, so handsome, so strangely calm. He has to go through with this charade that will last a lifetime. We agreed it was the safest thing to do, that it was for the best. I close my eyes because even though I want to hear, I can't watch him as he declares his love for Carina. I won't look at his mouth as it announces something that will tear us apart forever.

'I am grateful for my chance to speak,' he says. Now, hearing his words, his breeding is so evident, that I can't believe I never noticed it before. 'For many years, I stayed away from this place, afraid for my life. When I was young, I barely understood why I had been sent away from my family, from my city, from my friends, but a faithful servant explained to me the cause. Carina has offered a salve that will heal this festering wound between our families, and spare my life. For that I am grateful.' He pauses and draws a breath. 'But I am also ashamed, because I cannot accept.'

I open my eyes. Did I say what I think he did?

Carina tries to smile still, but her face has become flushed. 'Roberto . . .'

'To marry you would be the easy path,' he says, 'but I will not do so for reasons you know well. If my exile for all these years has not placated your father's anger, then I will happily do all in my power to seek reconciliation. But I will not run away any longer.'

She's shaking her head. 'This is a mistake. A mistake . . .'

He's stopped listening to her. 'Laura, where are you?' he shouts, like a man in the dark.

'Who's *Laura*?' someone says above the silence.

'I'm here,' I whisper, stepping out. One or two faces turn to me. 'I'm here,' I say more loudly.

Others turn and a path opens leading from me to Roberto. I see Paulina, her mouth opening and closing like a fish stranded on the shore. Nicolo's brow is creased.

Carina shouts over the rumbling of the spectators. 'I will not be humiliated!'

But Roberto jumps over the railings of the altar platform and bounds towards me. He reaches out his hands and I press against him. I hear the hammer of his heart.

'I don't care what happens now,' he says into my hair.

'Neither do I,' I whisper back.

37

The sound of a sword being drawn makes everyone gasp. Roberto puts a hand on my arm, gently moving me away from him. A woman screams and the crowd seethes in panic.

Another sword slides icily from its sheath.

Julius's armed guards stand either side of him, their eyes fixed on Roberto. The painted nobles back away.

Julius is mumbling, and at first I only see his lips moving. He's saying something over and over again. He grows louder: 'In my family's name. In the name of my family.'

I take Roberto's hand. I've made a decision. If Julius is going to have him killed, he can do the same to me. I don't care.

The Doge releases his wife's hand and moves until he's just a few paces from Julius. 'Friend, listen to what my son says. So much time has passed beneath the bridge.'

'You lied to me, to my wife, to this *whole* city!' He casts an arm wildly over the crowd.

'I lost my son,' says the Doge.

'But yours has been restored to you,' growls Julius. 'You have no moral authority here, Alfonso.'

The crowd gasp at the insolent use of the Doge's name, and

Roberto looks at me. 'Laura, this is very important,' he whispers, his words come quickly. 'You must walk away from me. Please, if it is the last thing you do for me, just walk away slowly and don't come back here. I'll meet you when all this is over.'

But I'm not stupid. I know what he's doing, and I have to make a choice. 'I won't leave you.'

'If you go now, then maybe both of us have a better chance.'

I stand in front of him. Julius's men approach closer and no one makes a move to stop them. My father gapes. I back away with Roberto until we're pressed against a wall.

'Enough!' shouts a voice.

Like goddesses from another world, Grazia and Allegreza, flanked by a flurry of women, move between the men. They hold up their arms. The gesture suddenly seems more powerful than any sword. Other noble women, many of whom I have only seen masked, peel off from their husbands and surround me and Roberto. The armed men hesitate, lowering their blades slightly. They don't know how to move through a shield of women.

Grazia stands in front of her husband and puts her hands on his chest. 'Julius. Julius. Julius,' she says. 'No murder in a house of God. No murder in this place.' Though her words are uttered quietly, they aren't a plea, nor a hope. She's giving an order. Roberto's arms enfold my waist. My fingers are white where they press into his arm.

Julius's face is hard and he sweeps his hand aside, which must be a signal for the swords to be sheathed once more. His men obey. The Duchess rushes over, her face grim and set. When she reaches us, she touches Roberto's shoulder.

'Go, my son. At once.' He looks at his mother and then at

me. 'Let go of her, I tell you.' She tugs my hand from his arm and points towards the choir stalls at the front of the chapel. 'You must run, before they kill you. Go!'

Still, he doesn't move. I take the ring off my hand, the twisted loop that matches Beatrice's, and I press it into his.

'Listen to your mother,' I tell him. 'There's no time.'

He seems to break out of his trance. 'I'll come for you,' he says, and then turns, running towards the rear of the church. He looks back once, then disappears.

I look around. Allegreza and Grazia are coming straight for me. They must know what I've done – what I've revealed to Carina.

I turn, but the crowd has thickened. I try to get out but I stumble over the fabric of my dress. I scramble to get to my feet and Allegreza and Grazia grip my arms, one on either side.

'Get away from me!' I shout, but I don't think anyone hears above the hubbub of the congregation. 'Leave me alone!'

I try to push them off and I'm strong, but they're stronger. They pull me aside, into a vestry off the main chapel. Jesus stares down from his cross, his head to one side, a look of passion and pain in his eyes.

'There's no need to fight,' says Allegreza. 'You must stop all this struggling!'

I snap with my teeth, trying to find her arm, and she lets go. Perhaps she'll pull a dagger from her dress, and push its point between my ribs. Perhaps I'll die here.

'You killed my sister,' I say, turning to Grazia. 'I know what you did. I'm not the stupid little girl from the convent you think I am. Not any more.'

The two women look at each other with an expression that I don't understand. There's even a smile on Allegreza's lips.

'What are you speaking of, child?'

'You killed Beatrice,' I say and jerk my head towards Grazia. 'I saw her giving money to the woman who wears my sister's ring – Bella Donna. I saw her do it, right beside the tomb of her son. I was watching.'

Grazia looks to the floor and brings her hands together in a solemn clasp. And I'm glad because I think she looks ashamed. It's a relief to confront them with the truth. No matter what happens next.

But Allegreza only looks more confused.

'A ring?'

A flicker in her face makes me feel less sure of myself. I tell her about my ring, and seeing it on the hand of a woman who could only be a prostitute, given the wanton way she was dressed, the fall of her wild hair. I tell them what I know, what happened that day in St Mark's. When I've finished, Grazia's high colour has faded. She shakes her head at us both and faces me.

'None of this is as you think it is, Laura,' she says. 'I know what you saw, but Bella Donna is no murderer. I swear it.'

'She may not have been the one who carried out the deed, but she acted as your go-between.'

'Our go-between with whom?' asks Allegreza.

Again, a look of wry incredulity passes between the women. If it's an act, they carry it off with aplomb. Suddenly, I'm not sure of anything. I wanted to stand and fight them, but a strange weariness creeps into all my limbs.

'Why should I believe you?' I ask.

'Because we are the Segreta,' she replies. It's an illogical response as far as I'm concerned, but strangely, it seems also to carry with it the weight of some deep and incontrovertible truth.

'I know that Beatrice came to you,' I say.

Allegreza lifts her chin and looks at me. 'Yes, she did. And if you want to know more, you will come with us.'

Against my better instincts I go with them, away from the chapel and the noise, which has dipped to a peculiar kind of masculine hum.

'Ah,' says Allegreza, 'I know that sound. It's the noise men make when a fight has been thwarted.'

Grazia puts her hand on my arm. 'You know, in an hour from now they'll all be drinking together in one of the taverns.'

Allegreza laughs. 'Yes, and they'll be pummelling each other kindly on the backs, telling stories about this day, delighted to be able to exaggerate them for the sake of those who weren't there.'

Their irreverent speech doesn't seem like the talk of murderers.

They take me to Allegreza's home nearby, her private chambers. A breeze blows through the salon and a wide bowl of fresh fruit sits on the middle of a round table. Three chairs, arranged in an arc, have been placed at the broad window overlooking the lagoon. Allegreza tells me to sit. I don't, at first, but once she and Grazia have taken their seats, I feel foolish, and so take mine.

'Beatrice did come to us,' explains Allegreza. 'The night that she died, she came to one of our meeting places in the city. Like you, she was in despair about her impending marriage to Vincenzo.'

So it wasn't Roberto she was visiting. I imagine my sister leaving Faustina that night, making her solitary journey through the dark streets. I wonder if she was as afraid as me.

'And you didn't help her?' I ask.

Allegreza shakes her head. 'The rules of the Society are strict and they're old. Beatrice had no secrets to reveal.' She lowers her eyes. 'So we could not help.'

She speaks matter-of-factly, and without callousness. Her words ring with a sad truth. I've stood where my sister did, and felt the masked faces of the Segreta drive me from the room. I turned back, of course, clutching my secret about the Doge like the key to my freedom. Beatrice had not, for the only secret she had was the one I heard myself from Cecile's lips. Beatrice *knew* about Roberto, but would not tell *them*. My eyes brim with tears, as I imagine my sister returning to meet Faustina at the bridge, burdened by her duty and a future with Vincenzo. Braver than I was, that's for certain. My poor, loyal sister, who would live unhappily rather than betray a secret.

'We are not without pity,' says Grazia. 'When the news of her death came to us, we were gravely saddened. Her misery must have run deep if she took her own life.'

I look sharply at her. 'My sister didn't kill herself. Someone attacked her, and took her ring.' I tell them about Faustina's terrifying ordeal, about the man with gold teeth in the shadows, who held her as Beatrice drowned. 'Someone took her ring, and now that woman . . . Bella Donna . . .' I look at

Grazia, expecting another confrontation but she does not frown or glower.

All she does is shake her head.

'Laura, Bella Donna is a good woman. You misunderstood what you saw that day.'

I think I've misunderstood everything. 'Then what did I see?'

Grazia takes a deep breath, then explains, in halting low tones, her sad connection to Bella Donna. It's nothing like what I expected. Her marriage to Julius was never happy, she says, but like so many couples in Venice, their union brought their respective families privilege and benefits. After only a few months, she became pregnant, and God blessed them with a son, Carlos. It was as he was growing up that Julius began an affair with the daughter of a respected Councillor. The poor woman became pregnant, and worse still, imagined she was in love. She managed to conceal the pregnancy from her family, but the Segreta intercepted a letter from her to Julius. Grazia wasn't angry, her own marriage was loveless. She felt sorry for the woman and sought her out. They became close, but then, fearing the shame of discovery, she disappeared.

'And she was Bella Donna?' I ask.

Grazia shakes her head. 'She was Bella Donna's mother.'

'What happened to her?'

Tears spring into Grazia's eyes. 'She delivered her child in squalor, then hung herself in despair.'

'And Bella Donna grew up on the streets?'

Grazia wipes the moisture from her face. 'For a time she was looked after by nuns, but she ran away. I help her when I can, and she helps me. In many ways, she's more a daughter than Carina.'

If only she knew the truth of those words. But I cannot bring myself to compound her wretchedness. I feel stupid too. If what she says is true – and I cannot doubt it – then I have misjudged her gravely.

'We can help you find your sister's murderer,' says Allegreza, 'but you must put your trust in us.'

I look out at the lagoon, and the shifting green waters. 'Do I have a choice?'

38

We drink a tea of camomile and lavender as the sun sinks like a golden ball behind the skyline. I tell them my father will be looking for me, and paint a picture of him rampaging through the house, filling the air with oaths and curses, swearing to lock his errant daughter away and rueing the day he released her from the convent.

Allegreza says that she'll take care of it, and writes a note to tell him I'm safe and under her care.

'That should keep Antonio from fretting,' she says, dispatching a servant to his house. 'We still have business to attend to today, and you're a member of the Society, so you should accompany us.'

'Is it a meeting of the Segreta?' I ask.

'Yes, of sorts,' Grazia replies, glancing at Allegreza. 'I'll travel ahead.'

After she has gone, Allegreza fetches my mask, retrieved, she said, after I fled the chapel.

'I thought I'd never wear it again,' I say.

She smiles enigmatically.

★

It is late by the time we leave the house, and as we walk together along the shadowed lanes Allegreza tells me that we're going to the house of Grazia and Julius. The house Carina grew up in. She outlines a plan to me that seems brazen and brave. After a short gondola ride in the darkness, two servant women meet us at the landing point and usher us inside. The house is similar to my father's, though more opulent, and in a downstairs room, which seems to be an office of sorts, the crowd of women have gathered in their masks.

Grazia beckons Allegreza and I to stand next to her and whispers to our escorts, who float away like ghosts.

'There are things tonight that need to be resolved,' she explains.

Allegreza, in a rare show of affection, places her arm on that of Carina's mother.

'It's a good thing we are about to do, Sister.'

Grazia nods. 'I've lost a daughter to madness, but I shall rescue my husband. Follow me.'

She leads the determined procession of women into the hall and up a curving staircase. Skirts glide like hushed sighs along the floor. It feels strange and voyeuristic for us to be invading the house like this. Grazia opens the door of a room upstairs. All is dark inside. Great curtains hang from the tall windows, muffling the snores of a man. A high bed swathed in netting dominates the room. And the large man who lies within it has none of the dignity or nobility of his dressed, coiffed, formal self. He's a great lump, rasping and drooling, unaware of the disturbance that is about to invade his repose.

'Wake up!' Grazia says from behind her mask.

Julius rolls over with a groan and a snort and she repeats her instruction, fierce now, and louder. He sits up, his eyes still closed. Slowly, he opens them, squinting and peering in the dark.

'Good God, what in the name of all that's holy ...?' he growls. His voice is sleep-thickened and shrill with panic. He struggles out of the bed, hauling himself to his full height. 'Who are you? How dare you? The middle of the night! What is your intention?'

'We don't wish to harm you, but you must listen to us,' says Allegreza.

'Claudio!' he bellows. 'Ricardo!'

'The servants have been dismissed,' says Grazia.

His face reddens with anger. 'My own wife comes to threaten me.' His fists clench and soften, clench and soften. If he resorts to violence, I wonder if we'll be able to stop him. 'Well – say what you have to say.'

Grazia clears her throat. 'You must forget the blood-feud with the Doge's family. You must declare an end to the threat on the life of his son.'

He laughs. 'I'm not lifting any vendetta just because my wife is telling me to. Take this coven of witches away before I have them dealt with.'

But Grazia is unruffled and purposeful. 'I'm not here as your wife, Julius. I'm here as a woman of Venice. You have two choices: lift the vendetta, or face public shame.'

'What shame?' he asks her. He's irritated and still sleepy, but there's a thread of nervousness too.

'Do you want me to tell the whole city about your penchant for your fellow Councillors' daughters? Do you want me to present the letter that Irina de Lombardi sent you all those years ago?'

'Irina de Lombardi?'

'You remember the name, I assume?' she says. 'But I wonder if you'd recognize your child?'

'It's a lie!' says Julius, but his voice falters.

Another woman comes forward from the crowd. She lifts her mask — a simple one, lacquered red and inscribed with swirling black lines. I gasp at the same time as Julius. It's the woman, Bella Donna.

'My mother left me in the cell of a convent the day she killed herself,' she says.

'Be quiet, woman,' he says, but he looks broken.

'Why? Everyone here knows that it's true. It's the secret that makes me belong to these women. You can't take it away. It's mine.'

I can almost see the struggle between Julius's public reputation and private rage play out across his face. And though his rage is still sharp and furious, he knows the women have won.

'Don't think that because I am your wife I won't bring your dirty secret into the open,' says Grazia. 'All that you've built, your businesses, your position on the Council – I'll watch them strip you apart.'

'You would do that?' he asks, incredulous.

'We have lost our son,' says Grazia. 'Our daughter is a stranger to us. Anger has brought nothing but grief.'

Julius sags on to the bed, suddenly just an old man again. He looks at the wall, and his breathing is laboured as if at any moment he will shout again. In his lap, he holds his fists clenched. I can imagine his thoughts: a mixture of shame, and fear, and anger. The taste of humiliation, but also the prospect of reconciliation. If he's anything like my father, he's wondering how he can turn this to his advantage.

Finally he looks at his wife again. 'Very well,' he says, frowning, 'I'll make a statement to the Council in the morning. I'll lift the vendetta if that's what you want. Now leave me alone. Can't a man get some sleep in his own house any more?'

We leave in silence. At the door, I look back to see Carina's father pull the sheets over his head.

Outside by the water's edge, the women disperse into the night like seeping shadows. One remains with Grazia at the doorway to her house, holding her lacquer mask and watching me intently. Bella Donna. Grazia nods to her, and the woman approaches slowly. We stand facing each other for a little while.

'I'm sorry,' I tell her, for there's nothing else to say.

Slowly, she slides the ring off her finger. Just a small object, but it has haunted my dreams and been the focus of so much of my grief. She hands it to me. I push it on my own finger and it nestles in place of the one I gave to Roberto. Twisted, golden, warm.

Grazia closes the door, leaving us completely alone.

'We call him "Golden Mouth",' she tells me, 'the man who gave me the ring. All the girls know about him. His teeth are capped with gold, and though he can be rough . . . Well, he pays for what he gets.'

I feel pathetic, and ashamed. For all my complaints, this woman's life has been beyond my worst imaginings.

'Where can I find this man?' I ask.

Bella Donna shakes her head. 'Even if I could tell you, I wouldn't. He's not a man – how shall I put it? – to be trifled with.'

'I think he killed my sister,' I say.

'Then he would kill you too,' she replies. 'I know him, and I know his kind: cruel, without conscience. He would think nothing of slitting your throat and finding the next merchant vessel out of Venice.'

We are both silent as her advice hangs in the mist above the water. Of course I can't bring such a monster to justice on my own, but my father could summon the city watchmen. They have weapons. They could overpower the golden-mouthed murderer.

'I'm not proud of what I've become,' Bella Donna tells me, gazing into the water.

I put my hand on her shoulder, and squeeze softly. 'You owed me nothing, and you've given me so much,' I say. 'I'll be grateful always.'

From my purse, I draw out three silver coins and offer them to her. They sparkle in the moonlight like fallen stars.

Bella Donna smiles. 'Keep them,' she says. 'You may need them more than I do.'

I watch her as her silhouette, a proud shadow, recedes into the night.

39

'Why didn't you say he was the Doge's son? You should have told me, you stupid girl!'

I'm tired of the walls of my father's house, each room a prison like my convent cell used to be.

No amount of telling him I didn't know seems to make any difference. I need to send a note to Roberto at once, to tell him that all is safe. That the sword hanging over his head has been sheathed.

'I banished the *Doge's son* from our home!' He runs his hands through his hair.

And as sick as I am of the walls that contain me, I'm sicker still of the 'yes, Father, no, Father' rituals that themselves have conspired to tether me. And though it may be wrong of me, and though I may let loose the dogs of his anger all the more, I'll tolerate it no longer.

'Oh, you're such a ridiculous man,' I tell him. 'Our house is crumbling and your fortune is gone and it's no one's fault except your own.'

Bianca has left a bowl of fruit on the low table beside him.

He picks it up and flings it at the wall. His tantrum continues as smears of peach and nectarine slither down the paint.

'I've had quite enough!' he roars.

'I can see that,' I say, trying to stay calm. 'Do you plan to hit me again?'

'I will have respect from you. Get to your room!'

I walk quickly up the steps, ignoring his angry footsteps clattering along behind me. I sit upon my ruffled bed. The door slams and I hear the twist of the key in the lock.

It's dark and I'm taut, sleepless, sitting by my window. The moon outside is full with pale compassion. He is out there somewhere, hiding in fear. I should be with him. Soon there's a soft knocking at the door.

'It's me, sweetheart.'

Faustina. I walk to the door at the same moment as the key turns.

It's a relief to see her kind face. We hug each other.

'How on earth did you wrestle the key from him?'

She smiles. 'Old Faustina has her ways,' she says, tapping the side of her nose. 'He's downstairs, so we must be quiet.'

'But he said I wasn't to come out until he said so. You'll get into terrible trouble.'

'Oh, darling,' she says, stroking my hair. 'The great wisdom of age is that you know when the time has come to break the rules. Listen, there's no time for idle chatter.' She rummages in the folds of her clothes and brings out a scroll. 'Here. It was delivered earlier.'

The seal is smeared and I can't decipher the crest. I break it open, but the writing too is alien to me. Whoever has written it was in a hurry for the letters are a scrawl. As I read, my deflated heart becomes full again:

My dearest Laura,
Come this instant, and don't consult with anyone. Come alone to a barge at Saint Lucia harbour, where I will be waiting for you.
    May my love bring you quickly.
    Roberto

'It's from him! He's waiting for me. I have to go.'

Faustina nods her head and smiles. 'Of course you do.'

In the candlelit dark of the room where I grew up, Faustina and I plan my escape. She leaves the room on tiptoe and returns with a bundle. I open it and a brown, male suit falls out of it.

'What? Is this for me?'

'They belonged to old Renato. You can't risk being seen by your father, or his friends. Go on, put them on.'

I struggle and wrestle myself into the strange clothes. Brown breeches pulled over my lacy slip. A white cotton shirt, rougher than the ones Giacomo my artist, Roberto my prince, has worn. A dark jacket, which I shrug on. I tuck my tousled hair up into a cap. I look in the mirror and laugh. I'm standing in my room, looking like a smooth-faced boy. In less than an hour Roberto and I will be together and there will never be a barrier strong enough to keep us apart again.

I cannot go down the main stairs, for fear of my father catching me, so Faustina and I fashion a rope of sheets. She tests all her knots, her old hands tugging sharply on each to make sure they're sound. She ties one end to the back of my chair and wedges it under the window sill. She pushes the window out and tosses the makeshift rope down into the garden.

'You know where you're going, sweetheart?'

Her words carry with them another meaning altogether. We both know that I might not return.

'Yes, I know.'

'Be careful, my love.'

She fixes the buttons of my jacket, and tucks a stray curl under my hat.

I climb down the rope, using the knots as footholds. My hands are burning by the time I reach the ground. The rope snakes back up the wall and I blow a kiss to dear old Faustina.

I keep my head down as I run. It might have been fun to be a Venetian boy. The streets are empty and silent except for the echo of my steps.

A lone man waits by a single gondola around the corner. He's very tall. His broad hat casts a circular shadow around his face and shoulders so that I can't see what he looks like. But still the sight of him warms me, for this is the man who is going to take me to my Roberto. My heart practically sings. I go up to him.

'Laura?' he mutters, his eyes flickering over my boy's clothes.

Roberto has sent him.

'Yes, yes, thank you,' I say, climbing into his gondola. It rocks in the glass-still water as I take my seat.

It's said that no one can tire of Venice at night. The sparkle and lurking beauty surprises you at every turn, no matter how many times before you've seen the city in the dark. As we pass under each bridge, and he stoops at the stern, I feel my happiness growing. Other gondoliers pass us and salute silently so as not to wake the sleeping citizens. *All will be well*, my mother's voice whispers. She was right, after all.

I can nearly feel Roberto's hands around my waist and his fingers combing my hair. My longing feels like a cherished ache, deep and delicious.

We are in a part of the city now that I don't recognize. I don't know the backwaters as well as this man clearly does; we must be taking some unfamiliar way to San Lucia. We reach the harbour.

A barge is moored to a great wooden post a hundred feet out in the sparkling water. It glows with faint lights. I strain to see Roberto on the deck, and wonder for a moment if he's even yet on board. As the swaying gondola cleaves the water, closing the distance between us and the barge, I make out glowing lanterns in stiff brass holders beside the oarlocks.

A stepladder hangs over the side of the barge and with an expert tug of his paddle, the gondolier brings me alongside.

'Thank you. Thank you so much,' I say again, and the light from the barge's lanterns flickers. There are candles, too, inside the small half-covered cabin. With my first foot on the step, the candlelight lifts the shadows under the gondolier's hat, and a grin spreads slowly across his face. My heart flutters, weak and frantic as a trapped bird. The grim smile widens and I see his teeth.

His golden teeth.

40

I pull myself aboard quickly, stumbling on to the deck, with my eyes fixed on the man I'm sure killed Beatrice. Now I recognize too the shape of his shoulders – he's the one who delivered Mathieu's tongue. Panic tightens my throat as new light falls into my dull memories. The man in the black hat, who seemed to be watching me . . .

Footsteps make me spin around, and the horror tightens. Carina steps out from the other side of the cabin, her hair wild and scattered, her gold and white dress torn. Her feet are bare. She glides over the deck like a ghost.

My stomach lurches as the truth becomes clear. The note! There was something about it. Something clipped and controlling that I should have seen. It could never have been written by him.

The golden-toothed man takes off his hat, and smoothes his hair against his head. He's the one who delivered Mathieu's tongue to us.

My mind flickers with broken options. Jump off the side? They'd have me in a second. Scream for help? They'd slit my throat. Fight back? Impossible. He cut out a man's tongue.

'Thank you, Chrixos.' Carina speaks as normally as if she were dismissing a servant from a dining room. 'Go now. Do as I have instructed you. Roberto will be waiting.'

I watch him push his boat away with the long oar, like Charon crossing the River Styx and leaving me on the banks of the dead.

'He's been following you for quite some time,' says Carina. 'To and from your secret little meetings.'

'Where is Roberto?' I ask.

Carina grins, her hands clasping within her gown. The air is chill here in this wide-mouthed harbour. She cocks her head and eyes me quizzically.

'You are dressed strangely, Laura.'

'Where is he?' I repeat.

'Roberto has gone to meet *you*,' Carina says. 'At St Mark's. Your beloved man, who you were so keen to ensnare, waits for you. He's in for a bit of a surprise. A simple trick, but rather clever, don't you think?'

I put my hands to my mouth. A little sob bursts out of me.

'Ah, the passion and torture of young love!' she giggles. It's a horrible, lifeless sound. 'You're a foolish girl indeed. And Roberto – so blind. But not to worry, I've sent Chrixos to open his eyes.'

'Why would you do that? What has he done to you?'

'What has he done? What has he *done*? He's humiliated me in front of the whole of Venice. He's deceived me by pretending to be that wretched painter boy. But I'm not a fool. I knew. I knew even before I lifted his shirt and saw the scar on that lovely chest of his. I knew before you left the convent.'

The serpent of grief stirs inside my body.

'You murdered my sister, didn't you? You did it because you thought he loved her.'

She talks with her lips curled. Sweat trickles down the sides of her face. Her fingers are twisting.

'She wasn't good enough for him. From my girlhood, my father had promised my hand to Roberto. It was meant to be, until all this . . . this *politics* interfered.'

'You can stop all this. You don't have to make things worse. Please let me go to him,' I beg.

She moves towards me. 'Let you go? I saved him. I looked after you. And how do you repay me? By treachery. If it weren't for you, this would have been so much easier.'

She lunges at me. A sharp heat rips through my shoulder. I cry out, and see a dagger in Carina's hand. She comes at me again, slashing wildly, and I fall back against the edge of the boat. The lanterns lodged on either side of the deck send light swooping and flashing. One of them falls with a smash.

As she darts, I grab the hand that I once held in friendship. I twist her wrist as far as I can. Shaking, clutching, praying. We grunt and pull, locked in a hateful embrace. She manages to turn the dagger, and its point trembles as she presses all her weight behind it, teeth bared. I think of Roberto. I try to pull up strength and purpose from within me. With a twist of my body, I throw her against the edge of the boat and the dagger skitters away across the deck.

Carina pounces, and her hands grasp my throat. I wedge my fingers under hers, trying to pull them away, feeling my breath caught in my burning lungs. I'm dimly aware of the flames climbing behind us, lapping over the wooden cabin.

'You bitch,' she spits. 'Calculating. Greedy. Vicious. Bitch.'

She pushes me and we both stagger backwards in some strange drunken dance. I fall hard on to the deck, and she lands astride me on her knees and locks her hands around my neck again. Black spots and flashes crowd my eyes. Is this what it feels like to die? Is this what Roberto too, will feel soon? My heart aches to think he might suffer more. Something presses into my back as Carina bears down on me, and I realize what it is. The dagger. I scrabble desperately underneath me and find the hilt. Carina screeches, pressing her claws harder into my neck.

I don't have much strength as I plunge the knife into Carina's dress, somewhere at her ribs, but she lets go of me, screaming and clutching at her side. I taste sweet air.

Her feet glow strangely and her screams of pain turn to something more animal and terrified. Her dress has caught in the flames. It licks quickly around the hem, then seems to leap, golden and alive, to her waist. A change in the wind brings a mouthful of smoke that leaves me bent over and coughing.

She wails and dances. She tries to run blindly, but only throws herself deeper into the furnace that has gripped the boat. I see her mouth, twisted amid the flames as her hair catches.

I am transfixed for a moment by this fiery goddess tossing out cries of rage and fear. But Carina cannot be saved. I will burn too if I stay for another second. I scramble to my feet and climb on to the rail of the bow. Carina's shouts float upwards into the air along with black flakes of ash from the burning boat. I jump.

The water brings a haven of sudden silence, but a heartbeat later, the cold seeps through to my skin. I burst up in a panic through the surface and look back. Carina's shouts have dimmed to pitiful moans as a section of the cabin collapses with a shower of red cinders. I start to swim, without looking back.

As soon as I reach the bank, I climb up the slippery side, dripping, sodden. I know which way to go. I run, driven by the hope in my heart that threatens at any moment to be overcome by looming dread.

Back streets, convoluted paths. My panic is like another person running beside me. A frightened companion, showing me the way as I rush headlong, terrified and panting to my destination.

And when I reach the crooked rectangle of St Mark's Square, I'm sure and frightened that it's too late, but I don't stop. The clock reads just after three in the morning, and no one is around to hear my steps. I should be cold, but the fire is still with me. I find the main doors of the cathedral closed and bolted. But not even the great portico of St Mark's will defeat me at the final hurdle. I run around to the side of the church. Sure enough, a small entrance is ajar, and admits me to the dark interior.

There's no light, other than that which comes from the moon through the windows.

'Roberto?' I whisper. I think I hear a noise, but it might just be the creaking of the door behind me. I patter quickly along the side of the nave, pausing for a moment at each column. The stillness of the place is like a solid thing. I think

I smell traces of Roberto, that mix of paint and wood. He's been here. But perhaps Chrixos is here too by now . . . I'm poisoned by a fear that I can taste.

The silence is broken by the bulky thud of echoing footsteps. The way the sound bounces makes it impossible to hear which direction they come from.

I scan the upper galleries. The saints in their domes peer back, deathly and merciless. Then, from across the nave, I see him. Roberto stands in the entrance to the chapel that holds his tomb, waving. 'Laura!'

A shape looms behind him. The monster is there, standing in the shadows, with his black cloak shrouding his shoulders like a giant bat.

'Run!' I scream.

It's too late. Chrixos rushes at him, and his arms lift above his head and slip something over Roberto's neck, dragging him back into the chapel. My beloved chokes and struggles.

I rush between the pews and into the chapel. Roberto is half collapsed, writhing as Chrixos pulls the garrotte tighter around his throat. I fling myself at the assassin, raking my nails down his face. He grimaces, releasing his grip on Roberto, and swings an arm at me. The back of his hand clubs my cheek and sends me crashing to the ground. I roll across the paved floor until my temple catches against the sharp pedestal of the tomb.

I'm dazed. Lifting a hand to my head, it comes away slicked with blood, thick and red. I stand unsteadily, using the tomb for support as the two men wrestle on the ground, grunting in a terrible knot of limbs. Chrixos rolls on top and his fist thumps into Roberto's face with a sickening crunch. He lifts his fist again, but this time Roberto manages to buck his body, and throws the murderer off.

I stagger dizzily against the wall of the chapel, where a white marble cross hangs.

'Help me, blessed mother of God,' I whisper, lifting it off the wall. It's heavier than I'd imagine.

Roberto has managed to stand, but pants desperately. Chrixos faces him and crouches, pulling a dagger from his boot. He advances, and the fingers of his free hand flex with anticipation.

I step up behind him, and as Chrixos turns I swing the crucifix like a mallet. The blow lands right on his forehead, with a crunch like stone hitting stone. He collapses to his knees and clutches at his face as blood pours between his fingers. When he draws his hands away, I see a deep gouge in his head. His eyes, blinking through the blood, are wild with rage. He grasps my wet clothes. I lift the cross high, and not daring to look, smash it down.

The crack of his skull brings bile to my mouth.

His hands loosen and I feel the weight of his head slump against my feet. Roberto throws his arms around me, and tells me not to look. But now I want to.

Chrixos lies still on the ground, his eyes staring in a silent anger. His teeth shine in his mouth like the shells of yellow beetles.

'Are you all right?' Roberto asks. A trickle of blood creeps down his neck.

An uncontrollable shaking has seized my limbs, but I manage a nod. 'I think so.'

He touches my face and my neck and my hair and kisses me on my forehead and my ears and my nose and my lips. I wince as his hand brushes my shoulder.

'You're hurt,' he whispers.

'So are you,' I say, brushing his neck with my fingertips.

But nothing can touch us now we're together, and we're safe.

41

Four days later

The boat, marked with the symbol of the key, takes me to San Michele once more. The lagoon is still, but for the shivering ripples caused by occasional gusts. Gulls wheel overhead with tearing cries.

My shoulder is healing quickly. The wound was deep, but clean, and though it is stiff I don't need to wear a sling. Allegreza summoned a doctor to her house at once that night after Roberto and I staggered there, arm in arm, not letting go of each other. The physician tended to me quickly and efficiently, and after he'd left – paid well for this service and his silence – the Duchess's cousin listened to our story patiently, told as it was in a weary, weakened haze. Though she must have realized, by Roberto's presence, that I'd broken my oath of secrecy, she didn't baulk at any time.

We land on the island, and I put on my mask, walking through the now familiar corridors of the monastery. The Segreta's business never sleeps.

My father was beside himself, of course, and, when he heard

that I had been attacked by bandits, he blamed himself as much as me. I had asked Allegreza how we should tell Grazia of Carina's death. Allegreza told me that the truth would serve no purpose in this case – Grazia and her husband need suffer no more. And besides, the boat sunk in the harbour belonged to her family; they would reach their own conclusions. So, between us three – two women and a man – we shared another oath. The circumstances of Carina's death are a secret I'm happy to keep.

We left Chrixos's body that night, lying beside the tombs, and Allegreza said she would find someone to deal with it before the watchmen were called. Since then I've revisited the spot. If I look closely enough, I think I see a stain of blood on the flagstones, but I doubt anyone else would be so observant.

I greet Grazia first in the meeting chamber. Her old frostiness is still there, but I've learned to recognize the warmth beneath. Roberto found it hard to fathom, at first, that the blood-feud that dominated his adolescence could be lifted as easily as we lift a rug to shake off the dust outside. But since yesterday, with Julius's speech to the Council delivered, his life is now his own to enjoy.

Once we have all gathered, Grazia takes away her mask, and the other women do the same. It's the first time I've seen all their faces at the same time. 'I want to be the first to offer my congratulations,' she says. 'Roberto will make a fine husband for you.' The other women approach too, and plant kisses on both my cheeks.

'Thank you all,' I say, slightly surprised – though I shouldn't be – that they know already. It was only the day before that

Roberto came to ask my father in person for my hand. I'm very much the favourite daughter now. He is having a new suit made for the wedding – 'From Pastollini, the finest tailor in Venice,' as he never tires of telling me.

We're all surprised to hear footsteps. Those who aren't already wearing their masks don them quickly. A young girl, perhaps younger even than me, creeps tentatively into the room, one hand still on the door frame as if she plans to run away at any moment.

Allegreza is in charge as usual. She shoos people out of the way to give the girl some space and tells everyone to be quiet.

'Are you the Society?' the girl whispers. 'The Society of Secrets?'

'Why do you want to know?' asks Allegreza.

'I need your help,' says the girl. 'And I have a secret to tell you.'

Sarah Dessen

Read her once and fall in love

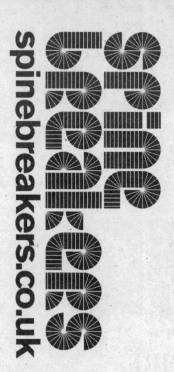